Reclaimed

A Central Valley Pack Novel
Book III

By:

Darie McCoy

Edited by: All That's Wright

Cover Art/Design: ASMcCoy

Inside Title Page: ASMcCoy

EBook ISBN: 978-1-961999-14-5

Print ISBN: 978-1-961999-01-5

For everyone who lost someone and fought their way back to living again.

"The most beautiful people I've known are those who have known trials, have known struggles, have known loss, and have found their way out of the depths."

— UNKNOWN

Author's Note

Hi. If you're new to my Central Valley Pack series, or you're one of those people who doesn't read story synopsis, you haven't met Rosco. Which means, you don't know about the tragic loss of his first mate and their unborn pup. This book delves into that loss as he is presented with the opportunity to be a mate and a father again. While it's not the entire story, this book does deal with grief, loss of spouse, angel baby, verbal abuse (mostly off page) and physical abuse (completely off page).

If either of those things are triggering or disturbing for you, I understand if you choose not to read further. If you think you'll be fine, I sincerely hope you enjoy Deanna and Rosco's love story.

Prologue

Rosco flopped over onto his back in the large bed staring at nothing on the ceiling. Faint hints of the rising sun filtered in through the window, and he knew he'd have to get moving soon. The sheets pooled around his waist allowing the cool air to float over his chest. He was surprised he hadn't kicked them off during his fitful sleep. That had been the case on many mornings when he'd actually managed to get a decent night's sleep.

Since...Millie...He didn't sleep as soundly anymore. He slept. But it wasn't usually what could be considered a restful sleep. Between his own thoughts and his wolf's melancholy, it was the best he could hope for. The beast barely spoke to him anymore, and when he did, it was in one-word sentences. Rosco guessed it was better than nothing.

His mama assured him it would improve, and one day he'd wake up not missing his mate so much, but Rosco didn't see it. Although, he'd gotten better at masking it. It kept the others from being overly concerned about him.

Pushing off of the bed, he trudged into the bathroom to get his day started. He had to meet Rahm for their morning run of a designated section of the pack borders, followed by a meeting with the security team. There hadn't been any reports of unwanted guests lately, but they remained vigilant.

By the time he made it to the edge of the forest behind the Alpha house, Rahm was already outside waiting, and the sun was fully in the sky.

"You're late." Rahm wore his usual scowl as he watched Rosco approach.

"I'm not late. You're early. What happened? One of the cubs bounce on your head to wake you up this morning?"

As the father of a set of twins and expecting a new addition in barely more than two summers, Rahm had a steep learning curve to fatherhood. Rosco was proud of himself that simply mentioning the cubs no longer caused a lance to his heart, reminding him of the pup he and Milly were expecting before she was so brutally snatched away from him.

Instead of answering Rosco's teasing question, Rahm simply shucked off his clothing and shifted into his bear. Following suit, soon Rosco's wolf was running alongside the big bear. With his wolf on alert, his nose tilted into the wind to pick up any unfamiliar scents. However, they encountered nothing unusual during their outing.

The only thing out of the ordinary to occur was the tug Rosco's beast felt when they came near the edge of pack lands bordering Cummings. While shifted, Rosco normally gave his wolf full reign. But, he was forced to intervene when the beast attempted to continue running past pack borders straight into the town.

Beast, what is going on with you?

We have to go there.

Go where? Cummings? Why?

*We **have** to go there!*

*Get yourself under control, beast. We have a job to do. We protect **pack** lands. There's nothing in Cummings for us.*

It took considerable effort, but Rosco kept the wolf on task. He and Rahm completed their inspection of the southwestern border and were back at the Alpha house in time for breakfast. Well, Rahm went inside for breakfast, Rosco waved off the invitation and went into pack town center.

As he was finishing up with Jeontugi and Aldis, Rahm came strolling into the office with Trip trailing behind him.

"Good, you're still here."

Rahm lowered himself into a chair as Trip grabbed one of the high-backed stools, flipped it around and sat in it backwards. Something about the way the two looked at him, put Rosco on edge. The other two members of the security team were smart enough to read the room and made a quick exit.

Tossing subtlety out of the window, Rosco quirked one eyebrow at Rahm and Trip.

"What are you two up to?"

"We've been talking." Rahm gestured between himself and Trip. Already on alert, Rosco sat up straighter.

"Have you been thinking as well, or just running your mouths?"

Rahm leveled him with a look which Rosco read as, 'Cut the bull-shit.' He was deciding if he wanted to heed the warning when Trip spoke up.

"You need to get away from this place for a while."

"What the fuck are you talking about? Like a vacation? Didn't we just get back from a little jaunt to Blacktooth Summit? Where else do I need to go?"

Trip lifted a hand in Rosco's direction while staring at Rahm. "See what I mean?"

"Yeah." Rahm scrubbed a hand over his face, then leaned forward with his elbows on his knees. "Other than to help out with Brody, and getting him moved back here, you haven't left pack lands in..."

Rahm's eyes darted away before coming back to Rosco. "You haven't gone farther than this office since before the twins were born."

While he artfully skirted the elephant, the big pink beast was still sitting smack dab in the middle of the room.

Folding his arms across his chest, Rosco leaned back into his seat. "I don't see the point. I've never been like you two. I don't have to hit the road at random times to do goddess knows what."

When Rahm looked ready to object, Rosco cut him off. "Don't give me any bullshit, Rahm. You haven't been anywhere lately. And the only reason you haven't, is because the last time you left pack lands you came back with a mate."

Swinging his gaze to Trip, Rosco let him have a taste of his ire. "And you. Who knows where the fuck you get off to for weeks at a time. You say it's for your transport business, but who's to say? And you know what? It's not my concern. You're loyal to the pack and come when we call. Why can't knowing the same about me be enough? Where the hell is this demand for me to take time off coming from?"

Rahm's face hardened. It was Rosco's indicator he was about to invoke his power as alpha. Part of him still wanted to fight, but Rahm's expression said it would be useless.

"You need a break away from this place. I don't care where the fuck you take it. You could go park your ass in the sand for all I care. But, come sundown, I don't want to see you on pack lands for at least two weeks."

As if he'd just uttered the words himself, Trip folded his arms across his chest to match Rosco's posture. *Fuck...*

Chapter One

Deanna 'DK' Madkins pushed the hair out of her face as she looked around at her handiwork. The new dining room at the Inn was a far cry from what it looked like when she first bought the place. While it wasn't completely run down, it was obvious it hadn't been updated in quite some time.

Now, the guests had a comfortable place to share the family style meals offered. When she'd purchased the bed and breakfast from Marigold, she was informed that Cummings wasn't a hot spot, but there was usually a steady stream of at least a few visitors per week. The pace suited Deanna just fine. She'd hired a cook and someone to help with the housekeeping, but they were only part time. Most of the load, she shouldered alone.

She was used to it. Her life before relocating to Cummings had been filled with her handling most things on her own. Despite being mated for more than ten summers, she was very self-sufficient. Barry was a wolf who prided himself on being a provider, but thought his job ended at the front door. In his home, he was to be king. Deanna shook her head, gritting her teeth remembering how much crap she put up with from that wolf.

A sudden infusion of happiness swept through her as the bad

memories were quickly replaced by the relief she felt after she'd gone to her pack alpha expressing her desire to set Barry aside. Technically, the phrase she used to Quinlin, was *set him free*. After more than ten summers as mates, Deanna hadn't gone into heat. Not once. It was obvious, especially to Barry that she was barren. If they remained together, their union wouldn't produce any pups.

As gruff and rough as Quinlin appeared, he was understanding of her plight. Although, it initially appeared she wouldn't have an ally in her unmated alpha.

Past

"DK, are you sure this is what you want to do?"

Seated in his office at the Alpha house, Quinlin peered at her with his far too perceptive amber eyes. Inside, her wolf paced, advising her to forgo asking permission and simply leave.

"It's what I need to do, Alpha. Barry wants pups. It's been more than ten summers. It's obvious I can't give him what he wants. Our mating isn't a fatal one. I know it's rare, but some mate bonds are severed."

Nodding, Quinlin folded his hands atop his ancient wooden desk.

"Yes, I'm aware that it's been done. Is this also what Barry wants? If so, why isn't he here with you?"

Deanna had held out hope Quinlin wouldn't ask about Barry's absence. Her mate was on one of his road trips. He worked amongst humans which meant he spent periods away from pack lands. If what he'd told her when he left held, he wouldn't return for at least three days.

"Barry is away for work. And to be honest, Alpha, he hasn't said he wants us to break our mate bond. But he has suggested we add a third. Someone fertile enough to give him pups."

The thunderous expression which took over Quinlin's normally stern face made Deanna want to shrink into herself, until she realized it wasn't directed at her. It was because of what she'd told him Barry wanted.

"He wants to add a third? Where would that leave you? As den mother to the pups from his new mate?"

"I suppose." Deanna was barely able to push the words between her lips. Her own anger rose the more she considered the insult her mate handed her with his suggestion.

"Deanna, thank you for coming to me. I know it took courage."

Deanna wouldn't describe the look he gave her as pitying, but it was a much softer expression than the one he'd previously worn.

"You need to know I'd never force anyone to remain mated—especially not under these conditions. Your petition is granted."

Surprised, Deanna sat up straighter, her jaw slightly unhinged. "We don't have to take it to the council?"

Shaking his head, Quinlin stood and walked around the desk. "No. All we need to do is discuss what you want to do moving forward, and I'll make sure it happens."

Present

That day was the start of Deanna's new life. Quinlin was more than generous in making sure she was financially secure enough to do whatever she liked. Unfortunately, he was the only one. It wasn't the pack members themselves, but Barry's immediate family and her own who seemed to take great issue with Deanna's choice. Not wanting to keep running to Quinlin every time something happened, she decided the best thing for her to do was leave Blacktooth Summit.

Striking out on her own opened up a whole new world. She'd bounced around to different places, exposing herself to things she'd never experienced. While she explored, she stayed clear of large shifter populations. She had no solid explanation why, she just did. After almost five summers of exploring the country, Deanna decided to settle in Cummings.

She'd been made aware there was a shifter community nearby, but made no attempt to join it. Even after hearing it was rumored to be a pack that welcomed shifters of all kinds, she wasn't tempted to explore within their bounds. She was content living in the small town which enjoyed the benefit of having the protection of the Central Valley Pack, when needed.

"DK?"

Deanna turned to look at the young woman who assisted her with housekeeping. Hannah leaned partially into the door, balancing with her hand against the doorframe.

"Yes, Hannah?"

"There's someone at the desk asking if we have any rooms available."

"Please tell them I'll be right there."

Giving the room one last sweeping gaze, Deanna stored the cleaning supplies she'd used and stopped at the small bathroom to fix her appearance. She didn't run a high-end resort, but she liked to be presentable when she interacted with her guests.

Stepping into the lobby, she tugged at the collar of her scoop necked top. It was short sleeved and relatively thin, but it suddenly felt like she was wearing the itchiest sweater she owned. All she wanted to do was get it off her skin. In fact. All of her clothing now felt too tight and restrictive.

A low growl thrummed through her, making her core clench and slicken. It took her half a second to realize the sound wasn't coming from her. Wide eyes searched the lobby for the source before landing on the wolf standing in front of the reception desk. He wasn't shifted, but even in her current state, Deanna recognized the scent of another wolf when she smelled it.

Actually, it was so loud, she wondered how she hadn't smelled him while she was in the dining room. The thought had microseconds to occupy her brain because her own wolf had risen up inside her. The beast's howling demands were loud inside Deanna's head.

Need! Need Now!

Need what, wolf?

Deanna wasn't certain if the wince scrunching her facial features was due to the demanding creature living inside her, or the near painful lust rampaging through her body. What the hell was happening? How did she make it stop? And why was the big, delicious smelling, wolf coming closer to her?

Thoughts of performing her duties were far from the forefront of her mind. Shifting on her feet, Deanna struggled to remain coherent and get her body to cooperate. But the heat was too much and the big wolf was getting closer. His stormy grey eyes were focused completely on her, making the thrumming in her pussy even worse.

She had to get out of there before she did something completely unprofessional. Taking a glance over her shoulder, she gauged the distance to the stairs. Going to her quarters wouldn't work. She occupied the rooms immediately behind the receptionist's desk. To get there, she'd have to walk past the dark-haired, broad-shouldered wolf.

"Don't." The single word was delivered in a growl from the unknown wolf.

"Um..." Deanna fought to stave off the desire clouding every part of her mind. What the hell was going on? "I'm sorry. Don't what?" Taking a glance over her other shoulder, she continued to weigh her quickly dwindling options.

"Don't run. If you run, I'll chase you. If I chase you, I *will* catch you. And, I won't be able to stop him from taking you wherever that may be. So, please. Don't run."

The rough quality in his voice sounded as if he delivered the words through gravel lodged in his throat. It was simultaneously menacing and erotic. Her body only cared about the second part. The moisture gathering in her core began to seep out. His silvery-grey gaze moved from her face to the apex of her thighs.

His tongue swiped his bottom lip before he bared his teeth in a feral grin.

"I don't know how much longer I can hold back. Where's your room?"

The haze of lust fogging Deanna's brain kept her from fully processing his question. But, when his fingertips touched the bare skin of her arm, she didn't care what he'd said.

Need!

Yes, wolf. Need!

Deanna agreed with her beast, launching herself at the unknown wolf, wrapping her legs around his waist and her arms his shoulders. His rumbling growl met her own as their lips collided. There was no way to know which of them initiated the kiss. Her mouth opened beneath his allowing his tongue entry to tangle with hers.

Large, warm hands cupped her ass, holding her tightly to his hard body. The feelings had relieved her of all sense of decorum as she wiggled in his embrace trying to find a way to alleviate the ache in her core.

"Please..." The request left her lips in a keening whine that Deanna couldn't control. It was immediately silenced by the wolf's lips taking hers again.

"DK?"

Only the heightened concern in Hannah's voice penetrated the veil separating Deanna from the reality where only she and the large wolf existed. Wrenching herself away from his drugging kisses, Deanna looked around.

"Hannah, just go. Take Owen and leave. Now!"

Human or not, Hannah's scrambling footsteps reached her ears soon followed by Owen's heavier tread. The bell above the front door tingled as it slammed closed behind them.

All the while, the wolf had his face buried in her neck. It felt like he was literally trying to devour her with the nibbling kisses he placed there. Her employees had barely cleared the door when a ripping sound rang out. Her shirt and bra were in tatters. The air from the cooling unit had zero effect as he lifted her up, quickly engulfing one turgid peak.

The suckling draw on her nipple ramped Deanna's desire up to indescribable proportions. Shame wasn't a thought as she began to actively beg for relief.

"Please. Please...!"

The cool surface of the wall met her back right before her loose pants met the same fate as her blouse. Her panties were no obstacle. Mid-plea she was filled to the brim with his thickness. All of the air escaped her lungs, and she summarily forgot how to inhale as his cock stretched her walls. She was so very full. But, not sated.

Instead of the relief she anticipated, the desire raging through her got even stronger. Her beast was howling with unbridled joy inside her while demanding more at the same time. Deanna and her wolf weren't normally at odds. This time was no different. She needed more. But the hulking wolf pinning her to the wall wasn't moving.

Driven by instinct, she used the tiny space she had to rock her hips, attempting to glide herself on his turgid length. Her movements earned her a sharp swat on her ass and a nip to her breast. His response only served to make her want him more.

The beast at least understood her message as he used his hold on her generous ass to tilt her hips aligning her perfectly to accept his thrusts.

He wasn't gentle. He gave no quarter as he conquered her pussy claiming every millimeter of it as his own. Caught up in the sensations ruling her, Deanna would've agreed to anything. So long as he didn't stop fucking her. He could growl whatever nonsensical words he wanted. So long as he didn't stop.

"Aahh!" Her orgasm overtook her with such force, her entire body locked around him.

Her nails ripped through his shirt, likely breaking skin. Her walls convulsed as the release rocked her. At that exact moment, Deanna felt the stinging prick of teeth on her shoulder, near the base of her neck. Another round of shudders wracked her as she was tossed into the abyss once more from the feeling. In all of her forty-five summers, Deanna had never felt anything like what she'd just experienced with the unknown wolf.

With each breath, her breasts pressed against his hard chest. Her tattered clothing hung on at odd angles, but he remained fully dressed. Limply, she collapsed into his sturdy frame. His body was firm, and...stiff. Almost like he wanted to be anywhere but there with his cock still pulsing inside her.

Lifting her head, Deanna looked into the face of the wolf who'd just left his mating mark on her shoulder and filled her with his seed. His handsome face held a look she could only describe as tortured. Tentatively, she trailed her fingers up from his shoulder to the hair at his nape, stroking him there.

"Are you okay, wolf?"

If Deanna thought he felt stiff before, his body became hardened steel. His wide-eyed stare was focused on her lips, before his brow dipped and darkness took over his features.

"What did you just say to me?"

Until he asked, Deanna hadn't realized the words she'd spoken in her head could be heard. Her eyes rounded in an exact duplication of his earlier expression. *Goddess help her*! The only way he could've heard her, was if they'd established a mate link. But all shifters knew only fatal mates shared that kind of connection. The new information stalled Deanna's mind. There was literal silence within her. Not even her wolf ventured to break it.

Chapter Two

Rosco held the woman in his arms, with his cock still imbedded in her scorching heat, wondering how the fuck he'd come to be in this position. In the summers since he'd lost his mate, he hadn't looked at another female shifter or human with desire. He didn't want anyone else. Yet, the first time he left pack lands alone, he pounced on the first female shifter he encountered.

Not only did he pounce, his wolf demanded he mark her—claim her as their own. And he did it. Rosco couldn't stop himself. It was like some other wolf had taken over his body. Her scent drove him crazy to the point he wouldn't have cared if they were at pack town center with every shifter watching, he would've fucked her and planted his seed inside her. Even now, as he held her against the wall in the lobby of the inn, his cock remained hard. He'd come, but his shaft was at attention waiting for the next wave to hit them.

But, he shouldn't be here. He shouldn't be fucking someone else. He damn sure shouldn't be leaving his mating mark. He'd left his *mating mark* on her and he didn't even know her name. Only her initials. DK. And only those because the young human he'd spoken to when he arrived used them when speaking to her. A sense of betrayal invaded his thoughts causing his entire body to tense. He was actively trying to get his limbs to cooperate and let her go when she started stroking the hair at his nape.

It was comforting. Her soft brown eyes were filled with concern as she stared at him. He read her expression almost as clearly as he heard the voice speaking to him in his head. *"Are you okay, wolf?"*

Everything inside Rosco came to a screeching halt. It felt like his eyes were going to bulge out of their sockets. The voice wasn't his beast. Which could only mean one thing. He hadn't just pounced on a random female shifter. This she-wolf was his fatal mate. He knew it, but didn't want to believe it.

"What did you just say to me?" Rosco tilted his head, peering into her face. To her credit, she appeared just as shocked as he was when the new voice entered his mind.

"You...you heard that?"

"Yes."

Her gaze flitted away from his as if she was having an internal debate. If she was, she wasn't sharing it with him. It's possible she was speaking to her own beast. While he'd seen it begin to happen within their pack, fatal matings were still rare. He should know. His bond with Millie had been stronger than most. But, when she'd been taken from him, he lived on. Also, they had a sense of the other's emotions, but they'd never shared a mate link where they could speak mind to mind.

DK finally looked at him again. Her eyes remained filled with awe and confusion.

"Could you? I mean. I'd like to get down please."

Her polite request reminded him that he still held her balanced against the wall with his cock buried inside her. The heat of embarrassment crept up his neck. Not just embarrassment. Shame.

Rosco avoided looking into her face again as he stepped away from the wall and lifted her off his erect length. The traitor was still ramrod stiff. It jerked in protest the moment cool air hit the tip. Gritting his teeth, Rosco ignored the complaint. Once she was on her feet, he dropped his disloyal hands from her body.

His digits flexed in want to touch her soft curves again. Instead, he ordered his feet to take another step back. With his stare fixed on nothing in a direction away from her captivating features, Rosco detected her movements in his periphery. Her footfalls were nearly silent as she inched away from him.

He didn't want to, but he had no control over the way he followed her movements as she walked across the empty lobby. *The lobby.* It might not be the middle of pack town center, but he'd fucked her in the lobby of a public establishment without care of if there were other guests. Hell, anyone could've walked in off the street. His thought was confirmed when she stopped next to the front entry and turned the lock, before disappearing through the door behind the reception desk.

Why are you standing here? We should be near our mate. She will have need of us again soon. Go to her!

Rosco ignored his wolf's question, observations and demand. Knowing DK was now his mate and fully accepting it were warring within him. He wasn't supposed to have another mate. Despite his mother saying thirty-seven summers was too young to declare he'd never mate again, Rosco had been firm.

His family never tried to push another available shifter on him, but the mothers of single daughters didn't show the same restraint. Only six months had passed the first time it happened. Afterwards, the not-so-subtle hints had increased until he became outright rude with his rejections. It was completely outside his normal jovial demeanor, and a far departure from the shifter they'd known.

The wolf inside him, spoke up again when Rosco remained rooted on the opposite side of the lobby.

Mate! Now!

His beast began the growling chant, making Rosco wish he could somehow mute the volume on their connection. The only good coming from the annoyance was Rosco became aware of his dick hanging out of the open zipper of his jeans. Wrangling the stiff length back into his pants took focus—especially when the beast scoffed, stating he'd be better off removing the pants.

Her scent, their scent, clung to him. It filled his nose and messed with his ability to try to distance himself from the moment. In truth, his beast chanting in his head wasn't needed. Rosco's primal instinct would prevent him from doing what he thought his heart wanted. There was no way he could leave. Not now. Not when they'd just begun the period of mate bonding. Especially not with her being in heat. If memory served him correctly, they had a maximum of thirty minutes before their natures forced them to couple again.

Even as the thought occurred to him, the potent aroma of her heat infiltrated his senses. It had barely been five minutes since the first time. Yet the scent was strong enough to reach him while there was more than half of the lobby and a closed door between them. Rosco's naturally keen sense of smell was amplified.

With his nose leading the way, his feet moved in the direction of the reception desk. Skirting the furniture, he pushed the door open without knocking. It was good that it was unlocked because he would've certainly torn it from the hinges if it had been.

His quick scan of the neat living room area was only in furtherance of his quest to get to DK. When he didn't see her, he stalked through the space to the next closed door. This one opened into a bedroom. DK stood on the opposite side of the bed framed in the doorway leading to a bathroom.

She'd shed the torn remnants of her clothing and was standing there bare. Her eyes were glossy, and her legs were squeezed tightly as if she were trying to hold herself together. The fragrant scent of her heat filled the room making Rosco's mouth water. Desire to taste her sweet nectar was nearly overwhelming. It was only surpassed by the drive to once again plant his cock in her velvet walls.

Stepping over the threshold, he ripped his shirt off over his head in one move. The rest of his clothing landed along the path he took to get to her on the other side of the room. When he was almost close enough to touch her, she held up a hand as if to stop him.

"Um... Wait. Please. I don't know what's going on. This isn't normal. The way I feel. This can't be right."

Her words were a plaintive cry for understanding, but Rosco knew the only thing which would help her, help him, was for them to continue with the heat mating. There was no other way around it. Closing more of the gap between them, he stopped when her outstretched hand was pressed against his bare chest. At the contact, her eyes closed and her nostrils flared as she inhaled deeply.

*"What is **wrong** with me? This can't be right."*

This time, when she spoke directly into his mind, Rosco didn't balk. Instead, he clasped her hand in his, moved it to the side and eliminated the final sliver of space separating them.

"There is nothing wrong with you. You're in heat."

"What?! That's not possible. I'm barren."

DK's assertion was followed by a moan. The heat would soon become painful, if they didn't do something about it.

*"I don't know who lied to you, mate. But you **are** in heat."*

"But they said...I thought..."

*"Shh...It doesn't matter what **they** said. I am telling you what is real."*

Touching her more gently than he wanted, Rosco battled to hold back in the face of her confusion. DK was a full grown she-wolf, but she appeared genuinely confused about the things going on with her body. Sliding his other hand up her arm, he ghosted his fingertips over the mating mark he'd placed on her shoulder. It was already beginning to fade.

Continuing, he wrapped his fingers around the back of her neck while using his thumb to tilt her head upward to his. Lust clouded her eyes keeping her lashes lowered halfway. Her breath came out in short pants through her full lips drawing his attention to them, making him wonder how they tasted. The appearance of her tongue wetting them broke his restraint.

Cradling the back of her head, he lifted her higher, capturing the enticing pillows and delving his tongue inside her mouth. One taste wasn't enough, he needed more. His eager mate appeared to have the same issue. Gripping his shoulders, she flung herself against him, wrapping her legs around his waist.

A low rumbling growl vibrated from his chest as he latched onto the rounded globes of her ass, guiding her as he glided his length between her folds. Their first coupling against the wall didn't afford him the best view of her plush body. This time, Rosco wouldn't be denied.

With two long strides they were next to the bed. DK squirmed in his arms, gyrating her hips, rubbing her pussy on his stomach leaving a trail of her heat scent—marking him in a different way. As much as he was

enjoying her mouth, driving his cock into her tight core was an impera-
tive. Disentangling her limbs, he dropped her onto the bed.

"On your knees."

She'd barely scrambled into position before he grasped her hips,
lined his cock up with her dripping center and surged inside. Slamming
his eyes closed for a moment, he savored the slick warmth engulfing his
thickness. Her snug walls stretched to accommodate him, but they also
seemed to undulate around his length. It was as if her pussy was milking
his cock for his seed. He was seated fully within her walls, but he
remained still.

"*Fuck...Mate.*" Unable to form words with his mouth, Rosco went
back to using their link.

"*Please. Please, wolf. Please fuck me. I ache. I ache so much.*"

"*Don't worry, Mate. I'll take care of you. I'll always take care of you.*"

Keeping his word, Rosco withdrew until just the tip of his shaft
remained inside. Her responding whine quickly morphed into a keening
wail as he pulled her onto his shaft at the same time as he punched his
hips forward burying his cock in her depths. The grip he had on her
hips was firm and bound to leave red marks on her golden-brown skin.
The thought of it only served to make him tighten his fingers as he
tugged her into his strokes.

Far too soon, her walls began to quiver. A gush of warmth preceded
a total lockdown on his cock. Her pussy gripped his thickness in a vice,
then undulated around him—once again reminiscent of milking him of
his seed. Rosco yielded to the sensation, spurting his release into her
waiting womb. His hips moved in lurching jerks as he pumped her full
of his essence.

Once he felt more in control, he flopped over sideways across the
bed. The springiness of the mattress caused him to bounce and brought
DK close to his side in a limp heap. It seemed so natural when she curled
into him breathing heavily. That was probably why it took him longer
than a few minutes for reality to seep into his psyche again.

"*Do you not want to be here, wolf. With me?*"

Already stiff and filled once again with remorse, a new feeling of
shame washed over Rosco. What he'd forgotten in his internal battle was
the things he'd learned from Rahm and Carleeta. Fatal mates couldn't

simply talk to one another mind to mind. They could feel the other's emotions as well. Obviously, his feelings of disloyalty had been transmitted to DK, and she'd interpreted them as he didn't want to be with her.

Rosco didn't know how to explain that it wasn't about her in particular. It was anyone. He wasn't sure he was ready to be with anyone who wasn't Millie. And losing himself in the instinctual mating with DK made him feel like he betrayed his mate. Except...DK was now his mate. As evidenced by the fading mark on her shoulder and the onset of her heat. She was his, just as he was now supposed to be hers.

Looking down at the beauty inching away from his side, Rosco winced from the cursing his wolf was giving him in response to the potential hurt to their mate. Wrapping his arm around her back, he rubbed her bicep.

"No. Don't. Don't pull away."

His wolf calmed down allowing Rosco to try to mend the hurt he felt from her.

"I'm sorry... DK." Frowning, he rolled the initials around in his mouth. He'd used them in his thoughts, but he immediately disliked them on his lips. "What is your name, mate? What does DK stand for?"

To his surprise, she giggled at his question. The giggles soon turned to outright laughter. Her mirth was contagious bringing a rare smile to his face. Goddess, she was beautiful when she laughed. Enjoying her glee, Rosco simply watched until the giggles tapered off to intermittent sighs.

"I didn't mean to laugh, but this situation is so ridiculous, I couldn't help it." Rubbing his chest to take away the sting of her words, she looked up at him. "Here we are, fully mated, and you don't know my name. And I have no clue what your name is either. Aren't we a pair?"

Holding on to the feeling of lightness brought on by her laughter, Rosco chuckled.

"You could say that, but you could also just tell me your name."

Captivating, dark brown eyes peered into his. "Deanna. Deanna Kathleen Madkins."

"Hello, Deanna Kathleen Madkins. I'm Rosco. Rosco Greywolf."

Chapter Three

The tingle in Deanna's belly had nothing to do with mating heat and everything to do with the wolf shifter she was cuddled next to in her bed. His voice was deep, almost decadent in its timbre. Before, she'd thought the intensity of the moment was the reason it sounded so low and gruff. While it held a harder edge when he first spoke to her, the overall appeal of it remained the same.

"Hello, Rosco Greywolf."

Looking around at her neatly appointed bedroom, she brought her gaze back to his. This definitely wasn't what she expected when she woke up to start the day. At forty-five summers old, and having been mated previously for more than a decade, Deanna was certain she was unable to heat and have pups. Yet, one sniff of Rosco Greywolf and her heat crashed on her like a tidal wave.

Earlier, she didn't possess the presence of mind to be embarrassed to not know her own body. Any female shifter of age to have offspring was taught what to expect when they went into heat. Deanna's only defense was the fact that she'd spent a considerable number of summers on the goddess's green earth without experiencing even a twinge of heat.

Being unable to produce offspring was an anomaly in the shifting world. For the most part, they didn't suffer from the ailments and afflictions humans dealt with. According to Deanna's own mother, no one in their line had ever failed to produce at least *one* pup. Thinking of her mother usually brought a sense of melancholy. This time was no different, only Deanna's sadness had a companion.

Despite her fit of giggles and Rosco assuring her that she wasn't the cause, she still felt sorrow and...shame she was certain weren't coming from her. She knew very few fatally mated shifters, but she'd learned enough to know their bond was deeper than other matings—that they were privy to one another's feelings and emotions. And Rosco, regardless of his assurances, was experiencing emotional turmoil.

Considering how his body had stiffened and she hadn't sensed any dread until she cuddled into his side, how could she not believe she was at the center of his confusion? Or at least a contributor. With determination, but without the sense of being unwanted, Deanna sat up. The move broke her tight physical connection to Rosco.

He continued to lay on his back. His gray gaze locked on her, and his brow dipped in question.

"I need to go check the log. There aren't any guests here currently, but there were a couple of pending reservations. I need to show all the rooms as unavailable for the rest of the week to keep anyone from booking."

When he sat up beside her, Deanna looked toward the windows to keep from staring at his sculpted physique. She especially didn't need to look at his cock, if she wanted to get anything done before the next heat cycle hit her. Regardless of her lack of experience with the process, she knew it could go on for days. Instinctively, she knew there would be no doubt when they'd planted a seed which would bloom.

Deanna felt the weight of Rosco's stare, but she didn't look at him. Instead, she left the bed, grabbing her robe on the way out to the computer at the reception desk. As she walked away, it felt as if his stare was burning a hole through the thin material covering her nakedness. Whether he wanted to be there with her or not, there was little doubt either Rosco, his beast or both appreciated her physical form.

Feeling his stare caused a stirring in her nether regions and she picked up the pace. She had a business to run and she didn't want to send it into the crapper simply because she was forced to yield to biology. Deanna also didn't want to run the risk of being ass up on the reception desk being mounted. The large windows at the front of the inn would give the entire town an excellent view of their pup making activities.

She'd barely clicked the last button to block all ten rooms when the throb in her core started up again. Her blasted heat hadn't even given her enough time to call Hannah and Owen to give them the rest of the week off. At least she hoped it was only through the rest of the week. She wasn't sure her pussy could take more than five days straight of Rosco's brand of coupling. It's possible their explosiveness was a symptom of them having a double dose, with establishing their mating bond along with a heat cycle. Something told Deanna it wasn't the case.

Crossing her legs, Deanna squeezed her thighs together and picked up the phone. If she could just call Hannah, she could get the young woman to pass the information on to Owen. She'd only pressed the first three numbers when the pulsing throb in her core caused her to fold, leaning heavily against the desk.

The sound of the door opening behind her penetrated the fog, but Deanna didn't turn around. Beyond the overpowering scent of her need, she smelled his woodsy aroma. The phone clattered against the desk when it tumbled from her fingers. Not giving it another thought, Deanna slid her fingers into Rosco's short strands tugging on them as he swallowed her moans with a kiss.

The coolness of her sheets did nothing to calm the heat blazing through her. Especially not with Rosco's big body pressing her into the bed.

"You let it go for too long. Again."

"I know... I'm sorry. Please. Please."

Deanna didn't care about Rosco chastising her for not returning at the first signs. She just needed him to fill her up. Stop the ache. Relieve the throbbing at her center by planting his seed in her womb. The concept of shame ceased to exist as she begged for his cock.

His hands cupping her breasts were an excruciatingly sweet torture. Swollen and sensitive, her nipples relished in the attention, but it only made the thumping heartbeat in her pussy louder, more demanding.

21

When he took one tender peak into his mouth and suckled, Deanna flew over the edge into an orgasm from the suction alone.

"Rosco!" His name was a scream in her mind and on her lips while her fingers nearly ripped his hair from the roots.

Lifting his head, Rosco released his captive only to capture her other turgid peak giving it the same treatment. Letting it go with a pop, he had her legs thrown onto his shoulders, with his cock invading her core before she could draw her next breath. Filling her completely in one stroke, he stole her ability to perform the basic function.

As much as her body demanded the invasion, it didn't lessen her desire. Instead, she wanted more. Tilting her pelvis into his pounding strokes, she met each one, driven by the need to satisfy the commanding ache.

"More! Harder!"

Deanna didn't recognize the she-wolf using her mouth to direct the shifter powering into her dripping core. The voice was husky, deeper, with an unknown rasp. Her mate required very little encouragement as he raised up on his knees, pressed her own to her shoulders and swiveled his hips, giving her every inch of his thickness.

Granting her request, he slammed into her depths. The slapping sounds were even louder than the grunts and moans neither of them held inside. Uncaring of any marks she might leave, Deanna's fingernails raked down Rosco's arms as far as she could reach as she was tossed over the cliff into a back bowing climax.

Cries to the goddess flew from her lips intermixed with choice curse words praising her mate's efforts. Rosco's thrusts became erratic as he soon joined her. Warm jets of his cum filled her channel to spilling, and Deanna couldn't bring herself to care. If she were honest, she reveled in it.

The beast within her was calm, and for the first time since she'd opened her eyes to start the day, Deanna went to sleep. She barely felt Rosco lowering her legs and leaving the bed. When she awakened, she was beneath the covers. Alone.

The lack of sunlight filtering through the window let her know it was now night, but she had to check the bedside clock for the time. Not allowing herself to consider what Rosco's absence meant, she rolled out of bed and went to the bathroom. Avoiding the mirror until she had no other choice but to see herself, Deanna rushed through relieving her bladder before stuffing her hair beneath a shower cap.

Knowing she'd likely be covered in the scent of Rosco and her heat soon, she didn't allow it to deter her from quickly bathing. Using the handheld shower head, she'd just rinsed the last of the body wash away and placed it back into its' cradle, when her mate's natural scent infiltrated the space. It carried with it the savory aroma of food, but Deanna's focus was on the masculine, woodsy fragrance she'd become addicted to in less than a day.

Looking through the textured glass of the shower, she could barely make out the muscular frame outlined in the doorway. But, she needn't have worried. Within the space of two blinks, she was face to chest with the big shifter who'd jump started her body into mating heat.

The dull throb in her core became a demanding thrum and slickness, not related to the shower, coated her inner thighs. Imprisoned by Rosco's stare, Deanna gazed into his eyes. Only desire was present. Nothing else. Their coupling, while short, was just as fierce as it had been each time they'd come together.

Once the last shudder of their release wracked them, they bathed. Some of the intimacy was lost when they performed the task separately, but Deanna tried not to let it bother her. Regardless of how swiftly shifter courtships normally moved, she knew next to nothing about her new mate other than his name and he was capable of sating her during a round of heat.

Their silence, as they went about cleansing themselves, was so loud, Deanna wished for noise, any other sound to fill the void. All that was there was the splashing of water against the tiles. At least the previous owner of the inn had remodeled the bathroom. So, they weren't bumping into one another as they showered. The space was large with two separate shower heads. Rosco had simply moved beneath the other one, allowing the water to pelt the top of his head.

Once she was done, Deanna made a hasty retreat from the enclosed space. Between her heat and their new mating, the compulsion to slam her private parts against his could strike at any moment. By the time she'd grabbed something to wear, she heard him exiting the shower as well.

Instead of the soft, comfortable pants she wanted to put on, she'd slipped a loose-fitting dress over her head. Considering what he'd done to the outfit she'd worn earlier, Deanna didn't want to chance him shredding any more of her clothes. The savory aroma from before hit her with more force when she stepped into the bedroom.

However, a quick inspection of the bed and nightstand didn't reveal the source. Despite not being able to see it, the smell kickstarted another natural body response. Hunger. Her stomach growled, reminding her it had been several hours since her last meal, and she'd burned a lot of calories since then.

"I got food from the diner across the street. It's on the table in the other room."

Deanna jumped. Even for a shifter, Rosco moved entirely too silently. Or was she simply that distracted? She couldn't say for sure. So, Deanna just nodded and left the room in search of something to quiet the rumbling in her belly.

When she entered the space, which doubled as her living room and dining area, she considered that she hadn't actually thanked him for thinking of getting food. There was plenty in the kitchen, but who knew how long they had before they'd go back to grinding their bodies together?

"I didn't know what you might like. So, I got a variety." Once again, Rosco's sudden appearance caused Deanna to jump.

"You're as skittish as a kitten, Mate." His voice held not even a hint of amusement.

Deanna watched him stride confidently into the room wearing only a pair of jeans. Not the one's he'd worn earlier which meant he'd brought extra clothing with him. It stood to reason, since he was attempting to secure a room when things took a turn toward carnal activities.

Not responding to his assessment, she simply lifted the lids on each container to view the contents. Deciding on the burger and fries, she sat in one of the three available chairs. Her stomach protested even more loudly as if the proximity of sustenance made the situation more dire.

When Rosco took the chair across from hers, she barely glanced up at him. Deanna guessed he noticed. Because, instead of opening a container to begin eating, he leaned his forearms on the table. She didn't have to see his gray gaze to know he was staring at her.

"Are you afraid of me?"

"No. Should I be?"

Her response was immediate and laced with the offense her wolf had taken at the implication. Her expression conveyed it as well. Deanna's gaze snapped to his face only to see a matching expression on his handsome features.

"You never have to be afraid of me. I'm your mate. I could never hurt you."

"Excuse me if that hasn't been my experience with mates. Besides, you still don't really want to be here with me. I can *feel* it."

Rosco's heavy lashes covered his eyes briefly before they lifted to reveal them again. "I—"

After a few halting attempts at him trying to speak to contradict her statement, she held up a hand.

"Don't bother to deny it, Rosco. You can't lie to me. Remember? One of the perks of being fatal mates. We can't lie to each other. Or did you miss that lesson in shifter mating education?"

In lieu of an answer, his jaw clenched and he slid one of the unopened containers closer to him. Deanna returned her attention to her burger as he dug into the short stack of pancakes with eggs, sausage and bacon. The diner served their entire menu all day. So, she wasn't surprised pancakes were among the options he brought for them.

They ate in silence. With her wolf being sated in more than one way, Deanna was able to finally call Hannah and Owen to let them know she was closing the inn for the remainder of the week. Promising to let them know if things changed, she avoided directly stating the reason for the sudden schedule modification.

They weren't shifters, but living so close to the Central Valley Pack, they had a rudimentary understanding of some aspects of shifter culture. Deanna didn't know much about the neighboring pack beyond what she learned from Leylandii, the Alpha Mother. The older shifter had accompanied Marigold anytime Deanna met with her prior to purchasing the Inn. She'd only seen the two of them sparingly since she'd taken over full time.

Mama Ley, as Leylandii insisted on being called, had invited Deanna to visit her diner in pack town center, but Deanna had never gone. Even with permission, it felt odd to trapse across another pack's territory.

After a solid thirty minutes of neither of them speaking and no new round of heat to make conversation unnecessary, Deanna finally broke. It was obvious Rosco was content to sit on the opposite end of the sofa embroiled in whatever thoughts were causing alternating waves of sadness, anger, and guilt to reach her through their link.

"Rosco Greywolf, where are you from?"

Chapter Four

So surprised, by not only the question but the fact that she spoke, Rosco snapped his head around to look at Deanna. Her neutral expression gave nothing away. He only knew she was apprehensive, because she couldn't hide those feelings due to their link.

"I'm from here. Well, near here. The Central Valley Pack. I'm beta to our pack alpha—Rahm."

"Mama Ley's son Rahm?"

Shocked yet again, Rosco tilted his head slightly, assessing her. "You know Mama Ley and Rahm?"

Her soft curls swayed gently as she shook her head. "I don't know them, know them. But, I've talked to her enough for her to mention her son. She came with Marigold to show me this place before I purchased it. I also see her around town on occasion. I've never formally met Rahm though."

Nodding, he lapsed into silence again. Of course, his beast didn't appreciate it. Not because he wanted all of Rosco's attention, but because Deanna's discomfort was obvious and Rosco wasn't doing anything to fix it. He wasn't even trying. Rosco wasn't relishing in her discomfort, but he didn't know how to fix it without making it worse.

She was right. He didn't want to be there. He'd only gone far enough from pack lands to technically be in compliance with Rahm's edict that he go away for a couple of weeks. There wasn't any place he had a burning desire to see. Also, seeing as it was spur of the moment, he didn't put any major thought into using the computer to find something.

Besides, if there was an emergency of some kind, in Cummings, he'd be able to respond much more quickly. Carleeta had talked Rahm into getting a set of cellular phones they were required to take with them when they left pack lands. It allowed them to keep in contact better, but Rosco didn't want to risk it being hours before he could reach home, if they needed him. At least that was the lie he told himself when he chose the small town a lion's throw from CVP lands.

You're causing our mate distress.

His beast, and constant companion, growled the statement. Rosco heard the warning without it being issued.

I'm not doing it on purpose, Beast. You act like it's easy for me to just take up with the she-wolf.

She is our mate! Her sadness is our sadness. Fix it!

I don't know how! What am I supposed to tell her? Hey, no offense, but I'm still mourning my dead mate. And I'm sorry, but it fucks with my head to now be mated to you. I'm sure that will go over really well.

Rosco wasn't even sure his wolf understood his feelings in such complexity. At his core, the beast lived by instinct. Until recently the sorrow over Millie's loss was shared, but his wolf had been restless for months now. The feeling intensified when he parked his truck in front of the inn. Once he got his first whiff of Deanna, his wolf had followed nature's course. Rosco was incapable of resisting the compulsion to plant his seed deep inside her.

It was only afterwards that the feelings came crashing down. The thoughts telling him he'd betrayed his vow to Millie by being with another. It strengthened when he heard the first tentative notes of her sultry voice speaking directly into his mind. The rush of elation at what it meant was immediately crushed by the guilt. It nearly broke him to experience such a connection with someone other than the little coyote he'd mated as well as married in a human ceremony.

Navigating those emotions while simultaneously being a slave to the mating bond had Rosco in a state totally foreign to him. It was no wonder his wolf was giving him shit. He was at war with more than one facet of himself. His wolf had quieted, but Rosco knew it didn't mean the beast was done with him.

After answering his question about Mama Ley and Rahm, Deanna had once again fallen silent. This moment of quiet was just as uncomfortable as the previous one. In his periphery, he noticed her rocking in her seat as if preparing to stand. Over their mate link, her hurt and frustration layered itself on top of what he was feeling.

Knowing he'd likely fuck it up, Rosco tossed caution aside and released his question in a huffing breath. "Where are you from, Kit— Deanna?"

He didn't know where it had come from, but he'd nearly called her Kitty Kat. From her expression, she caught the slip, but ignored it.

"I'm from the east coast originally. The past five summers I've traveled all over and lived in a few places."

It was odd for a shifter to be without a pack. So, her answer intrigued him—especially with her being an unmated female. It was dangerous in more than one regard. Concern furrowed his brow as he looked at her.

"What about your pack?"

Shame, which didn't belong to him, traversed their link.

"I left my pack after getting permission from the alpha to break the bond with my former mate."

Rosco's ears twitched at hearing she'd been previously mated. His beast growled, and Rosco struggled to keep the sound internal.

"You've been mated before?"

The gruffness in his voice was the best he could manage considering the way his beast was pacing in his mind at the thought of another touching her.

Glancing at him without turning to fully face him, Deanna nodded.

"Yes, but it wasn't a good mating. For either of us."

"What did he do?"

Innately, Rosco knew it wasn't something she'd done. Despite his reluctance to fully accept their bond, her being the cause of her failed mating was immediately rejected.

"It wasn't him exactly. It was me. Or at least I thought it was..." Deanna averted her eyes, chewing on her bottom lip for a beat before looking at him again.

"I told you earlier that I was barren. I believed it fully because after being mated to Barry for more than ten summers, I hadn't gone into heat. Not once. Not even a twinge."

Rosco's beast made it to understanding at the same time he did. "He blamed *you* for not producing a pup? It never occurred to him that he might be the problem? Considering our current situation, he most definitely was."

Shrugging, Deanna looked away. "For all we know, it could've simply been the goddess's will for me and Barry not to have pups together. He had a new mate before I left Blacktooth Summit. They could have half a dozen pups by now."

"Asshole."

The insult was mild compared to what his beast contributed to the conversation. Deanna hadn't said it, but the pain she'd experienced in her previous mating lingered. Rosco sensed it through their link and it fanned the flames of his anger. Barry of the Blacktooth Summit wolves should give thanks to the goddess Rosco had no knowledge of any of this when he visited their pack lands a few months prior.

He didn't meet many members of the pack during the little excursion, but was certain he hadn't met a wolf carrying the name Barry. It was Rosco's only consolation for not taking the time to beat his ass for causing Deanna distress. It didn't matter that he hadn't known her at the time, or his current reluctance to fully embrace their mating. The idea of anyone hurting her didn't sit well with him.

Of course, his internal deliberation of her situation with her previous mate, made him feel more like the asshole he'd declared Barry to be. She was bound just as much as he was by the dictates of the goddess. Yet, she wasn't trying to distance herself from him. Not the way he was holding himself apart from her. Knowing it and correcting it required a skillset Rosco wasn't sure he possessed.

Nature gave him a reprieve when a fresh wave of Deanna's heat scent invaded the soundless barrier between them. Rosco's nostrils flared, inhaling the decadent aroma of her desire. He couldn't say if him or his beast was responsible for the growl rumbling from his chest. Instead of jumping or shying away, Deanna met him halfway in the center of the couch as he practically lunged at her soft form.

That round and the ones which followed, were frenzied and rough. Rosco had bouts of guilt for handling her so coarsely, but the way she responded was a testament to her acceptance and enjoyment of their coupling. Having her ride him, while he ate up the view of her quim swallowing his cock, was an indescribable feeling he wasn't sure was completely due to her heat.

On the morning of the fourth day of their mate bonding and her heat, Rosco was pounding into Deanna from behind as he had her leaned over the very table they'd taken their meals on. They'd barely finished breakfast before he swept the food to the floor because the fragrance of her need was too much to bear.

"Yes, please. Yes. More. Harder."

Deanna's pleas were sent over their mate link while moans pushed from her swollen lips. Swollen due to the nips and kisses from Rosco as he was compelled to attempt to devour every inch of her. Their joinings prior to this one had been vigorous, but this time felt different. With a fistful of her hair, he tilted her head back, leaned over, and swallowed her moans while adding his groans to their sexual symphony.

Holding her hip in a punishing grip, he snapped his own, sending his length inside her as deep as physically possible. The tingling at the base of his spine was followed by his balls drawing up. A pinch to Deanna's nipple drew a strangled scream as her walls clamped tightly around his length locking him inside her. Her orgasm was a catalyst for his own. Grunts, gasps, groans and moans intermingled as their bodies continued to jerk together in the final throws of their mating passion.

When Rosco collapsed over Deanna's prone form, sucking in deep inhales, it felt as if his beast rolled onto his back squirming with glee. A moment later, the shift in her scent told the story. His seed was planted. Their mating heat was complete.

On legs which felt like rubber, using arms heavy as anvils, Rosco lifted Deanna. Walking through the bedroom, he took her straight into the shower. This was an established routine. Although his wolf considered it an affront to rinse away his essence from Deanna's body, Rosco performed the task anyway.

Drowsing in his arms during the process, his mate fell asleep the moment he pulled the covers over her voluptuous body. Looking down at her, he didn't understand why the compulsion to gaze upon her hadn't faded. The heat cycle was complete. His insatiable draw to the she-wolf should have calmed down.

The periods between heat sex over the previous few days had been awkward at times, and he only had himself to blame for it. His new mate was actively trying to get to know him, but they spent much of the time with him avoiding discussing anything about himself, beyond his role within the pack structure.

Most of the time, when they talked, he shifted the subject to her and how she'd spent the past five summers as an unmated shifter living among humans. It continued to be a subject of confusion and concern for him. Typically, the electronics and other devices humans surrounded themselves with, were enough to drive a shifter crazy. Their enhanced hearing picked up much of the sound waves others couldn't hear. Only prolonged exposure and training would allow a shifter to tune out the noise.

Rosco guessed it was the former and not the latter which permitted Deanna to live a life with humans instead of seeking out a new pack. Either way, there was now an entirely new situation they'd both have to navigate. He was certain the only reason there hadn't been any guests when he showed up was because it was the start of the week and weekends were typically the busiest times for small bed and breakfast places like the Inn.

Deanna shifted beneath the bedcovers, but didn't fully awaken. Her movements brought her closer to where he sat on the side of the bed. Once she was pressed against him, she released a sigh before settling back into sleep. *Why had she done that?* It felt as if she needed physical contact with him to sleep peacefully.

In her new position, her covered stomach was less than an inch away from his hand where it rested on the mattress. Without consulting him, his fingers inched closer until they weren't simply grazing her belly. His entire palm rested against her abdomen as he stared at the area in wonder. Just as uncontrollable as the movement which placed his hand on his pup's first home, were the emotions crashing into him, battering his senses.

While not totally the same, he'd been here before. With Millie. Only that pup perished along with his mate. He'd lost his budding family in one cruel moment. Jerking his hand away as if he'd been scalded, Rosco popped up from the bed. Not stopping once he was in motion, he grabbed his bag, tugging out the first shirt and pants he encountered, and hastily dressed.

It was too much. Everything was just too much, and the walls were keeping him from breathing. He had to get out of there. The gripes and grumbles of his wolf sounded off immediately, but Rosco pushed past them. Speeding away in his truck like there was an angry mob on his tail, Rosco disregarded his alpha's orders and headed back to pack lands. Away from the sleeping she-wolf and the torturous feelings ravaging his psyche.

WHAT THE FUCK ARE YOU DOING!

Shut it wolf!

I will shut it when you tell me why we are leaving our mate with our pup in her belly unprotected. Go back! Go back NOW!

Rosco winced against the physical pain elicited by his wolf's anger with his decision. Nothing about it was logical. If he'd been thinking clearly, he would've considered how it would be impossible for him to stay away from Deanna. They weren't just mates. Mates could be away from each other for more than a few days at a time.

But fatal mates couldn't. It caused them literal pain to be away from one another more than a day. Especially when the female shifter was carrying a pup. The instinct to protect was too strong.

However, instinct was at war with the other emotions Rosco hadn't fully dealt with following the vicious loss of his mate. How could he be happy about having a new mate and pup as if Millie and the pup they were expecting never existed?

Driving without considering where he was going, Rosco pulled his truck to a stop in the curved driveway in front of the Alpha house. Rahm's furrowed brow and the grim set of his mouth should've made

Rosco put the vehicle in reverse and leave. Instead, he opened the door and stepped out.

Stopping a few feet away from him, Rahm stared at him for a moment. Then, his gaze swept the cab of Rosco's truck. It only took a second for his scowl to deepen.

"What the fuck did you do, Rosco?"

Shame coated Rosco's every movement as he looked away from Rahm's accusing stare and shrugged.

"No. You don't get to show up on my doorstep four days after I sent your ass on vacation, smelling like a newly mated wolf, but I don't see a fucking mate in that truck. So, I'm gonna ask you one last time. What the fuck did you do?"

Leaning against the grill of his truck, Rosco ignored the heat against his lower back the same as he did the continued complaints of his wolf in his head. He accepted the pain attached, but did nothing to fix it. He didn't deserve to be comfortable. Instead, he grudgingly told Rahm about his intentions to stay at the inn in Cummings and his subsequent meeting and mating with Deanna.

And, for the first time, he admitted he wasn't completely okay. When he was done, Rahm was leaning against the front of the truck as well.

"I knew you weren't alright, but Beloved said I shouldn't push. So, I didn't."

This time when Rahm looked at him, Rosco didn't mistake his sympathy for pity as he'd done before.

"Rosco, I can't begin to understand how it feels to lose your mate. So, I won't try to speak to that. What I can speak to is what you're doing now. You're the fiercest wolf I've ever met. Yet, right now, you're being a coward."

Bristling under the insult, Rosco stood up straight. His body tensed as he stared at Rahm in disbelief. "What did you just say to me?"

"I didn't whisper, and I won't back down. You're being a coward running away from your mate when she's most vulnerable and only thinking about yourself. How do you think she's gonna feel when she realizes you're gone, she has *your* pup in her belly, and she has no idea where you went? What kind of mate are you? What are you expecting?

That she'll come chasing you down to beg you to be with her? Are you wanting promises that she won't try to take Millie's place?"

Up until then, Rahm hadn't actually said Millie's name. Mentioning her, while unbraiding Rosco in a way his wolf couldn't articulate, Rahm made him feel lower than the shit caking the bottom of a farmer's boots. Rahm uttered not one lie and gut punched Rosco without once raising his fists.

"I—" Rosco's reply was cut off.

"I nothing. Get your ass in that truck and go back to your mate. Fucking talk to her instead of holding all that shit inside."

Chastised worse than when his mama caught him pilfering Old Man Richardson's chickens, Rosco rounded the front of the truck and climbed back in. His wolf was absolutely zero help as he agreed with Rahm one hundred percent and didn't care how Rosco felt as long as they were headed back to their mate.

Although Rosco didn't need the two of them to light into him. He already felt like his chest was caving in. The further he drove away from Cummings the feeling got worse. When he was no longer able to feel Deanna's presence it became nearly unbearable.

Chapter Five

Deanna's eyes popped open with a start. For a moment, she simply lay there trying to figure out what woke her so suddenly. When she didn't come up with anything, she rolled to her side and closed them once more. The sheet lightly rubbed her skin, providing warmth but not the stimulating sensations of the past few days.

The absence of the demanding sexual undercurrent not only forced her to lift her eyelids, but to sit up in bed with her hands pressed to her mid-section. A sense of awe settled on her as she recognized the change in her own scent just as her wolf confirmed it. The first heat of her life was complete.

No visit to a doctor would be necessary to give the final seal. Nature had equipped Deanna with the innate understanding of her body— even if she'd discovered she was in unchartered territory. Besides, she wouldn't go to a human doctor and she didn't know if the CVP had a pack doctor.

It was when her thoughts drifted to the pack, that Deanna became acutely aware of the silence in her rooms. In their time together, Rosco didn't make much noise. Aside from when they coupled, or she asked him a direct question, he didn't talk much. But, the quietness wasn't the same as him being in the next room brooding.

"Rosco?"

Tentatively reaching out through their link, Deanna whipped the covers back and stood up. As an afterthought, she grabbed the garment on the ottoman at the foot of the bed. Holding it up to find the opening to slip it over her head, she realized it was Rosco's t-shirt. His woodsy, masculine scent invaded her nose as the cotton skimmed her body. The shirt was long enough to double as a short dress due to Rosco's height. But, Deanna's curves meant she wasn't swallowed by it.

There was no reply from her mate, and by the time she made it to the center of the front room, she understood why. He was gone. As sure as she knew her toes were scrunched against the tight weave of the area rug in her living room, she knew Rosco was no longer in the Inn and likely not in Cummings. She had no idea if mate links had limits based on physical distance, but she couldn't feel him. Not at all.

Panic unlike anything Deanna had ever felt collided with her normal calm demeanor. What did it mean if she couldn't feel him? Even though he'd exuded a constant undercurrent of indescribable, sort of sad, emotions the majority of the time, not feeling him at all was extremely disconcerting. The joy she'd felt only minutes ago when she'd realized she was with pup, was becoming a distant memory as she came to terms with her situation.

If she detected the difference in her scent, Rosco had as well. From the beginning, he hadn't been able to hide the fact he didn't want to be there. Deanna figured once he was certain her heat cycle was done, it was safe for him to leave. Somehow, coming to that conclusion hurt worse than all the times Barry had tossed out snide remarks about her getting older and never going into heat.

The emotional pain lanced through her, folding Deanna in half. Crumbled into a ball on the floor, with her arms wrapped around her middle, Deanna tried to remember how to breathe. How? How could someone she knew virtually nothing about have such a hold on her in less than five days? Deanna had no answers and her wolf wasn't any help. The beast was just as much if not more distraught than Deanna at Rosco's absence.

She knew he wasn't simply across the road at the diner. When he stepped out to get them food, she could still feel him. Where his energy resided in her for the past ninety hours, she felt nothing. And feeling nothing was a devastation Deanna wasn't prepared to handle. Rejection. That's what she felt. And it eclipsed any emotional pain she'd experienced in her first mating.

Our mate has left us?

It appears so.

Her beast's question wasn't delivered in her normal take charge manner, but in absolute disbelief. It was unfathomable. Yet it happened. Silent tears were her companion for an unknown amount of time before exhaustion forced her to sleep again. She didn't fight it. It was what her body needed after the recent demands made on it.

Deanna came awake, not to the hard carpeted floor she'd fallen asleep on, but in the last place she thought she'd be. In Rosco's lap with his arms wrapped around her, keeping her tucked against his chest. While her beast was inside her elated, Deanna stiffened against his solid frame.

Turning in his embrace, she didn't look up at him. Instead, she grasped his wrists, unwrapping his arms from her body. His grunt of protest was ignored when she stood. However, the moment she tried to walk away, she found herself locked in his arms again. His feelings of remorse weren't hard to read over their link and in his body language, but Deanna didn't want them.

"Let me go. Please." Deanna refused to look at him when she made the stilted request. She couldn't. Something told her if she looked into his tortured gray eyes she would simply crumble. No. Against her beast's objections, she tugged at his arms again.

Rosco's words were muffled against her abdomen, but Deanna heard him clearly. "Please, Mate. Don't walk away."

"Why shouldn't I? You did."

His wince from the hard edge of her words made her want to retract them, but she didn't. She was done silently accepting mistreatment from her mate. Her life was tethered to his. She wouldn't spend the remainder of the days the goddess gave her, biting her tongue and playing nice.

"I had a mate. Before you." No longer muffled, but delivered lowly in his deep tone, Rosco answered her question with his surprising declaration. "I had a mate before you. We were expecting our first pup. But, something terrible happened and they were taken from me."

The shroud of sadness surrounding him, made it impossible for Deanna to remain stiff—holding herself apart. Her fingers found their way into the silky hair at his nape and the tight muscles of his upper back.

"Taken from you?" As she asked the question, she wanted to call the words back as understanding doused her with sympathetic feelings.

"They were killed."

"Oh, Rosco..."

Her empathetic response joined his words which sent a sorrowful wave through their link. What he'd revealed put his conflicting emotions into perspective. Deanna had left her mating with Barry by choice. And she was happy to be rid of him. So, she felt no remorse for succumbing to the mating heat with another shifter. Despite Rosco being unknown to her when they first mated, a spark of joy was lit inside her when it happened. Until then, it had been her plan not to seek another mating, but to live out her days alone.

Rosco hadn't been so fortunate. He didn't get to decide to leave his mate. She'd been taken from him. Deanna delivered light, soothing, strokes to his nape.

"When did this happen?"

"Two summers ago."

Two summers? On one hand it had been two trips around the sun. On the other, it was recent enough to still be a little raw. Even though she'd wanted to be shot of Barry, it had taken her nearly two summers to stop expecting to see him when she returned to her temporary home each day. He'd been ingrained in her daily life for over a decade.

"What was her name? How long were the two of you mated?"

Rosco pulled back, but didn't release his hold on her. Deanna looked down at him with a questioning expression.

"You don't have to do that, Deanna."

"I don't have to do what?"

"Ask me about her. About our life together."

Bringing her hands around, Deanna cradled his face. "Yes I do." Curling her fingertips into his beard, she lightly scratched. "Now, tell me her name."

Rosco's gaze was steady, but his lips never moved as he supplied the name of the mate whose death had created a dark hole in his spirit.

"Millie. Her name was Millie."

"Millie. That's a sweet name. I bet she was a sweet person."

Deanna noted the marginal widening of his eyes in surprise at her assessment. She simply nodded in encouragement for him to continue.

"She was. Very sweet. A coyote shifter from a large family." Rosco's hold on Deanna tightened briefly before he loosened it a bit.

Deanna read his expression and the emotions he couldn't hide through their bond. He still didn't think she wanted or they needed to discuss Millie. He was wrong.

"Rosco, I'm not in competition with Millie."

A confused frown lowered his thick brows over his eyes turning them from gray to nearly black.

"Why would you say that?"

"Are you going to tell me it isn't part of the reason you left me? Or tried to leave me? Because you thought being my fatal mate, not hating me, meant you'd betrayed her somehow? That you'd chosen me over her just because you weren't still missing her every second of the day?"

The way he withdrew was the answer he didn't have to verbalize to Deanna. She'd located and pierced the heart of the situation, and her new mate wasn't certain how to respond. She didn't push. Thinking to give him space with his thoughts, she attempted to step away again.

Rosco's hold immediately tightened. His behavior contradicted the way he'd been prior to his brief disappearance. Before, he only got close to her when it was time for them to mash their bodies together trying to make a pup. Now, it seemed as if he *had* to have her near him. Not just near him. Held tightly against him.

"If I admit it, will you stop trying to leave me?"

"I'm not trying to leave you. At least not the way you left me."

The words escaped her thoughts before Deanna could censor herself. She meant them, but she didn't mean to actually say them—

even over their link. But, it seemed using the mate link resulted in lack of control when it came to keeping her internal thoughts private. The way he stiffened said they hit their mark, and she immediately felt guilty for piling on to his already raw emotions.

"I'm sorry." Rosco's gruff tone was filled with a depth of sentiment, conveying the fullness with those two words. "I shouldn't have left you that way. No matter what was going on with me, you didn't deserve to wake up alone with no explanation."

Leaning back, he tugged until she let him arrange her on his lap again. The rough pads of his fingers skimmed her skin gently as he rubbed her arm and bare legs. Deanna didn't say anything. She neither accepted nor rejected his apology. Intuition led her to remain quiet. Let him get it all out without interruption.

"You're right. I did feel like I'd betrayed Millie. Not just because I'd mated with another. Because...for a second...I was happier than I'd ever been in my life."

Deanna's breath caught and it took every ounce of self-control she possessed to restrain herself. Inside, her wolf was practically glowing from hearing him say it was his happiest moment. The beast had ignored the rest of their mate's tortured statement.

"Millie and I were mated for almost ten summers. I'd never had the desire to join my life with another before her. So, when she was gone, I didn't think I'd have anything close to those feelings again. Then, I walked into this place and met you. I didn't know how to handle it.

I still don't. Until my alpha found his mate, I'd only met one other fatally mated pair. My parents. I never imagined it would happen for me. After Millie and I married, I didn't even think about it. My life was good. Then, it wasn't. How was it okay for me to feel such joy and desire another so much?"

Deanna had no answers for him. Rosco's experience was one she couldn't relate to at all. It wasn't as if she'd never encountered a shifter who'd survived their mate and joined with another. She had. But, most male shifters moved on from their departed mates pretty quickly. Some even had more pups with their new mate if she was within the age to continue to heat.

The way Rosco held on to Millie emotionally, spoke to more than his love for his deceased mate. There was something else driving his guilt —keeping him locked inside whatever happened two summers ago.

"Rosco, I know you don't expect answers from me. And that's good, because I don't have any. Other than to know the goddess brought us together for a reason. Our lives are now tied to one another."

Turning, Deanna straddled his lap with her hands resting on his shoulders. Peering into the depths of his eyes, she spoke.

"There's nothing either of us can do about the past. But, what I can assure you of is this, you don't have to be alone again. Ever. I am your tether to this life—just as you are mine."

The cloudiness and uncertainty in Rosco's gaze lifted. A different warmth flowed over their bond settling in Deanna's chest. Whatever was going on in his head, he wasn't sharing. But the emotional weight he carried, had lifted—even if it was only by a small amount. It was enough to give her hope.

"I don't deserve you." Rosco stared at her with wonder.

"Well, it's a good thing the goddess doesn't give out blessings based on what we think we deserve. Isn't it?"

A corner of his lips tipped up, allowing Deanna a glimpse of a smile. Aside from the fierce expression he wore when they coupled, she'd only ever seen his face set to neutral or brooding. So, she and her beast lapped up the hint of contentment when it was presented.

A low rumble entered their discussion drawing a chuckle from Deanna. It seemed her stomach was demanding to be filled now that it was no longer tied in emotional knots. Tapping Rosco's shoulders, she made a silent request to be released.

When she stood, he immediately joined her drawing a slight smile to her face. It appeared he was willing to let her go enough to stand, but not enough to not follow where she went. Holding out her hand, she waited for his fingers to close around hers.

"I'm going to the kitchen to see what I can whip into a quick meal. Join me?"

Before Rosco could answer, his own stomach issued a complaint. It appeared when he'd left earlier, food hadn't been involved. An appreciative shiver glided along her arm, when his hand clasped hers. Still wearing his t-shirt as her only covering, Deanna led him across the lobby of the Inn, through the dining room and into the kitchen to find something to put in their bellies which didn't come from Main Street Diner.

Chapter Six

In his lifetime, Rosco had gone from being the eldest in a family of five, living in their oversized log cabin, to being mated to Millie living in the tiny two-bedroom home she asked for to be closer to her family, to existing in the same little house alone. Now, he sat in a large tufted chair in the lobby of an inn owned and operated by his new mate.

Five days had passed since he'd done what he admitted was one of the dumbest things in his life. While it appeared Deanna was understanding and forgiving, neither he nor his wolf were quite as lenient. In fact, the more he got to know her, the worse he scolded himself for leaving her alone for a few minutes, let alone almost an hour.

What is this nonsense?

A corner of Rosco's lips tipped up at his beast's question. Staying out of Deanna's way, unless she asked him for something, he'd taken to watching the television mounted on the wall. There was a movie playing. Although he hadn't watched many such things, Rosco recognized it as horror.

You know what it is, beast. It's a movie.

Is that what they think we look like? What the fuck is that thing supposed to be?

I don't know, beast. I guess.

It's insulting.

Rosco couldn't disagree. His mental shrug was accompanied by a real one as he repositioned himself in the seat. Shifters had lived out in the open for longer than Rosco had been alive. Yet, humans still insisted on making movies depicting wolf shifters as werewolves. Which didn't exist. And it seemed wolves took the brunt of the blasphemy as he hadn't heard of any movies featuring werebears or weretigers. Those must not have the same appeal for human entertainment.

As it happened often when he wasn't right next to her, Rosco's gaze found Deanna where she stood behind the reception desk talking to Hannah. She was teaching her how to run the computer system she'd installed to help streamline the business end of operating the Inn. As if she felt his eyes on her, Deanna looked over at him. The tiniest lift of her eyebrow asked the question before she pushed the words into his head.

"Do you need something?"

*"No. Do **you** need anything?"*

"No. If you're sure..."

"I'm sure, Mate."

Looking back at the computer screen, Deanna pointed to it as she resumed her training with Hannah. The reason for the training was fresh in his mind as they'd just discussed it two days prior.

Two days ago

Rosco tracked Deanna's movements as she went about her nightly routine. He'd already done a perimeter check and made certain the property was secure. Now, he was waiting for her to finish getting everything set for the next day. Three of the ten rooms had guests—two couples and a man traveling alone. All were passing through, using the inn as a stopover point to their destination.

"All done."

Slapping her hands together like she was dusting them off, Deanna smiled. The action pushed her rounded cheeks higher making her eyes look like they were almost closed. He, once again, thought he didn't deserve her. That he'd been gifted with a beautiful mate, not once, but twice was incomprehensible.

As she approached, he couldn't stop himself from appreciating every aspect of her beauty. Her medium brown skin had golden undertones which made it seem like she was glowing, while her hair grew out and up from her head resembling a lion's mane—only with fat curls. Her full lips reminded him of his new obsession with kissing. The end of their mating heat hadn't dulled his desire to fuck his mate. Rosco didn't know if the craving would ever diminish, and based on her response to him, he didn't think it bothered Deanna at all.

Slipping his arm around her once she was within touching distance. Rosco pushed open the door behind the reception desk being certain to engage both locks behind him. The door wasn't sturdy enough to keep out a shifter, but it was strong enough to deter the average human.

The cellphone, he finally remembered to bring in from his truck, started to ring. Rosco released his hold on Deanna to grab it from the bedroom.

"Hello?"

Instead of a return to his greeting, Rahm's grumpy voice came over the line. "I take it since you didn't come back, and I haven't heard from you, that you fixed things?"

"What are you, my therapist now? I'll go see Doc Portia if I want my head shrunk."

"Stop avoiding the question. Did you fix it?"

"What are you doing, fishing for gossip? Yes, I fixed it." Darting a quick glance at the open doorway, he muttered, "mostly."

"What the hell does that mean?"

"It means I'm alive, and I'm working on it. Bye, Rahm."

As he pressed the button to end the call, he heard the grouchy bear threatening to kick his ass if he hung up in his face. It didn't stop Rosco from tapping the icon and placing the phone face down on the nightstand.

"Is everything okay?"

Deanna walked into the bedroom, but didn't stop until she was standing in the doorway leading to the ensuite bath.

"It's fine. Rahm was just checking in. First, he tells me he doesn't want to see my face for two weeks, then he calls like he can't go more than two days without talking to me."

With a light chuckle, she leaned against the door frame. "Well, maybe he can't. Have you ever been away from pack lands for this long? I know you technically aren't far away, but you're not in his backyard either."

"I'm not in his backyard when I **am** on pack lands." Rosco walked closer to her as he removed his t-shirt and tossed it aside. "But, I rarely go away. The last time was for almost a week to help out another pack member. I wasn't alone though. It was a group of us."

Backing into the bathroom as he advanced on her, Deanna nodded. "Oh. Well, there you have it. I'm sure the last time you kept in closer contact since you were on a mission of sorts."

"Mhm."

Rosco reached for the edge of her top when she backed herself into the double sink vanity and had nowhere else to go. The rest of their conversation was delayed while they yielded to the ever-present desire pulsing between them.

Later, as they lie tangled beneath the sheets, Deanna revisited the subject. Her soft fingertips traced idle patterns on his chest as she snuggled close with her head tucked beneath his chin.

"Where do you live on pack lands? We haven't really talked about it."

They hadn't talked about it, because Rosco had been trying to work out the logistics in his head. He couldn't take Deanna back to the home he shared with Millie. Besides the fact that he lived there with his previous mate, it was literally next door to Millie's parents. He got along well with them, but he didn't want to appear as if he was rubbing his new mating in their face. Even if it wasn't what he was doing.

"I'd been living in the home I had with Millie. But I think I'll have to finally take Rahm up on the offer to move into the place near the Alpha house. It's larger and has more privacy."

Rosco tightened his embrace when she shifted in an attempt to sit up. After a beat, he released her just enough for her to connect their gazes.

"You don't have to move because of me."

"I'm not. At least not completely."

Giving her the shortened version, he explained why he was living next door to Millie's parents instead of the home normally occupied by the pack beta. Once she laid her head on his chest again some of his apprehension faded.

"If I were her parents, I can't say how I'd react."

In their short time together, Rosco had learned Deanna wasn't a particularly confrontational individual. She would stand up for herself, but her first inclination wasn't to tear off heads or rip out throats—be it verbally or literally. He really didn't want to find out if she could be pushed to those extremes.

Although, if he were anywhere nearby, they'd never learn that particular limit. He'd rip out throats and tear off heads long before she got the chance.

"That's not something I want you to worry about. I'll handle it."

Silence settled between them for a moment. Rosco knew she wasn't asleep, and he wasn't even close to being drowsy. Knowing he needed to be the one to say it, didn't stop him from taking a few extra minutes. It seemed unfair. She was just settling into her life, and here he was asking her to leave her new home. He would be leaving his, but the little bungalow he'd shared with Millie wasn't his place of business.

Just as it would be difficult for her to run the inn from pack lands, it would be hard for him to perform his beta duties if he was always in Cummings watching over his mate. The experience Rahm had with Carleeta, when she and Millie were kidnapped weighed heavily on him. The mate link had limits. Cummings was outside the range.

In theory, he could commute daily or she could commute. But it would drive him and his beast insane to be unable to feel her for hours on end. It had only been six days since they joined for the first time and already he knew he wouldn't survive it.

The day he'd left her sleeping, Rahm had simply reinforced what he already knew when he told Rosco to get back in the damn truck. Being out of range to feel his mate—especially while she was pregnant with their pup—wasn't an option.

"Deanna, I know it's a lot to ask of you..."

"Don't Rosco. It's the way of things. I accept it. We'll just have to devise a way to make it work for both of us."

He didn't think he'd transmitted his innermost thoughts to his mate, but she sussed them out anyway. Hugging her closer, he listened to her breathing until it evened out, indicating she was asleep. Until the Sandman took him, Rosco started a mental checklist of things which needed to occur before they could officially take up residence in the Beta house.

· · ·

Present

Once they'd made their decision that night, Rosco had reached out to Carleeta the next morning. Ignoring Rahm's grumbling, he asked if she could help with getting things together for the move. There was a sub council of sorts who helped in these situations if asked. Rosco didn't want much from his other house beyond his personal items and clothing.

Thankfully, Millie's mother and aunt had cleared the majority of her things out a few months after her death. They said it was to help him heal not having to see her clothes hanging in the closet alongside his. He didn't argue because they had a point. At the time, he'd taken to not hanging anything in there to avoid opening the door.

Rosco didn't want to move Deanna into an empty house. So, he'd let Rahm know he'd be extending his time away to give them an opportunity to get what they needed. The plan was to take her to see the place to have a look around first. Then, they would purchase the necessities and have them delivered before they officially took up residence.

Glancing at the window, he checked the angle of the sun. He rarely wore a watch since he could tell time accurately from the sun's position in the sky. It was nearing lunch which tracked with the aroma's coming from the dining room.

Deanna tapped Hannah on the shoulder before both moved away from the reception desk. Deanna approached him while Hannah continued on through to the dining room.

"I think Owen cooked enough for us to eat here if you want."

As if they'd done it thousands of times, Rosco spread his legs for Deanna to walk into the open space.

"I already told Mama Ley we'd come to the diner for the midday meal. If we don't show, she'll be out front before the sun goes down."

Plucking at the front of his plaid button down, Deanna nodded. She didn't ask, but he knew what else she wanted to know.

"My mama and sister are going to meet us at the Beta house. I don't want to overwhelm you..."

"We're shifters, Rosco. There's no such thing as half measures when it comes to this stuff. I know the drill. Everyone is in everyone's business without even trying to be."

Her knowing smile drew out a ghost of his own before he tapped her hip and guided her back a step so he could stand. They were ready to leave a few minutes later. Hannah would be staying over as part of her new role. Deanna had put a notice on the community job board for a third employee. But no one had contacted her yet.

The drive from Cummings to CVP lands was spent with Deanna tossing out the occasional question based on what she was seeing from the window. He learned once she was informed of the pack and their location, she had made a point not to drive in that direction out of respect for their boundaries.

Her statement made him wonder what would've happened if she had. She'd purchased the Inn and officially moved to Cummings a little over a year ago. Although she'd visited twice in the months before coming to a decision. As fucked up as he was at the time, it was a good thing he wasn't aware of her presence. Even now, he was still certain he wasn't deserving of her.

Pack town center was unusually crowded for a fall day, early in the week. Rosco didn't make eye contact with any of the shifters gawking as he shut off the engine, rounded the front of the truck, and helped Deanna from the vehicle.

"Hey there, Rosco." His nose told him what his ears heard was true. Millie's father, Glenn, was walking toward him wearing a wide grin.

"Glenn."

Rosco acknowledged his former father-in-law with a nod. Reflexively, his fingers tightened around Deanna's. Glenn's eyes moved from Rosco's face to his and Deanna's joined hands, then back. They asked the question he didn't voice.

"Glenn, this is Deanna. My mate."

Rosco abhorred the wave of anxiety he sensed from Deanna through their link. It felt as if she wasn't certain he would claim her in front of others. There was no way for her to know who he was introducing her to, as he hadn't mentioned names when he told her about Millie's parents. But the flash of surprise Glenn wasn't able to hide was likely a clue.

"Oh. Um. Well, it's very nice to meet you, Deanna. Welcome to the CVP." Despite his shock, Glenn's greeting seemed to be genuine.

"Thank you. Nice to meet you as well."

Clearing his throat, Glenn returned his stare to Rosco. "Sally said you'd gone off on vacation. I didn't believe her until I didn't see you around the house for more than a week."

"Yeah. Rahm's idea."

With a quick glance at Deanna, Glenn looked back at Rosco. "Well, it looks like it was a great one."

Something on the other end of the sidewalk caught his attention, and Glenn quickly shifted gears.

"Well, it was very nice meeting you, Deanna. Rosco, I'll be seeing you around." With that, he took off in the direction of the general store.

Unsure what put a fire beneath Glenn's feet, Rosco shrugged and guided Deanna toward the door of the diner. As soon as they stepped over the threshold, Mama Ley was there to greet them.

"Hey, Rosco! I thought I might have to come looking for you." Expecting one of her exuberant hugs, Rosco was shocked when she nudged him aside and tugged Deanna into her embrace.

"Hello, sweetheart! It's so good to see you again! Come on over. I kept a booth available for you."

As she hustled them through the restaurant, Rosco ignored the curious stares and outright sniffing from the shifters at the counter and other tables. He listened with half an ear as Mama Ley went on about how great it was to have Deanna join the pack. He'd expected her to introduce herself—since she'd taken the task from Rosco the moment they arrived. Then he remembered they'd already met.

They were seated in their booth with Mama Ley telling Deanna about the special of the day when the door to the diner banged open. All eyes were on the individual framed in the doorway. Sally. Millie's mother stood there stone faced with a posture implying she might shift at any moment.

Fuck.

Chapter Seven

Deanna followed Rosco's gaze to the opening of the diner. She didn't recognize the woman standing there, but from her posture and the furious glare she aimed at Rosco, Deanna had an idea.

"Sally! Sally, you come back here!"

Glenn, the man Rosco had introduced her to earlier appeared behind her. Neither of them confirmed it at the time, but Deanna had picked up on the context clues and figured out he was Millie's father. Which made the woman, pummeling Rosco with her facial expression, Millie's mother. And, she apparently wasn't as pleased as Glenn that Rosco had a new mate.

"Don't try to stop me, Glenn. I knew you were hiding something. Turning me around trying to keep me in the general store."

Jerking her arm away from him, Sally stomped a path through the tables heading directly for them. Deanna looked to Rosco. His face was a hardened mask. Sally was brought up short when Mama Ley turned and stepped into her path.

"Is there a problem, Sally?"

Mama Ley looked down at the much smaller woman. Sally's scent marked her as a coyote shifter, and she was significantly smaller than Mama Ley in height and build. Even if Sally chose to shift, which it looked like she was on the verge of doing, she was unlikely to be a match for the other woman. Mama Ley was a bear. And in true Mama Bear fashion, she placed herself in front of Deanna and Rosco, blocking Sally's access.

"No problem, Leylandii. I just want to talk to my son-in-law."

"Your son-in-law?" Mama Ley folded her arms beneath her ample bosom, but didn't budge from her position. "Oh. You mean Rosco. I don't think that's such a good idea. I can tell you came in here spoiling for trouble. And you know how I feel about trouble in my establishment." Taking a step forward, she backed the smaller shifter up a few steps.

Deanna's eyes widened, then nearly popped from their sockets when Rosco stood up. Using their link, Deanna tried to understand his intentions.

"What are you doing, Rosco?"

"I'm going to take Sally and Glenn outside and talk to them. I should've done it before now. Maybe seeing us wouldn't be such a shock if they'd been warned."

Mama Ley didn't turn around or even look over her shoulder, when Rosco rested his hand there.

"Maybe we should go outside and talk." His gaze was on Sally and Glenn. While Glenn readily agreed, Sally shook off the suggestion.

"No. Is there something you need to say that you don't want this harlot to hear?"

The rumble from Rosco's chest was so loud any murmurs of conversation throughout the diner stopped. A pin dropping on cotton could be heard in the silence. Anger radiated off him. Deanna could feel it without the use of their mate link. Yet, when he spoke, his voice was deceptively calm.

"Sally, you're upset. It's your right. But you **will not** speak of my mate like that. ***Ever.***"

The 'are we clear?' was implied at the end of his declaration, but it was heard just the same. Despite the tension of the moment, Deanna felt a rush of warmth from Rosco immediately defending her—especially from a woman he'd considered family.

"Rosco, I'm sure she didn't mean it. Her feelings just got away from her. Isn't that right, Sally?" Glenn's face was flushed red as he attempted to play peacemaker between his wife and Rosco.

Deanna deduced they were married in the human way based on the rings they both wore. Shifters didn't normally subscribe to such things, but her nose told her Glenn wasn't a shifter. He was human. So, it's likely they adhered to his custom in one aspect, but lived amongst her people.

"Don't speak for me, Glenn. I said exactly what I meant. My Millie's not even cold in the ground and he's already mated to some wolf no one's ever met."

"Get out."

His voice was low, but forceful when he spoke. The Rosco who'd attempted to make peace was fully absent. The ripple across his shoulders let Deanna know how he was struggling to control himself. Without thought, she slid from her seat and stood beside him. Slipping her hand into his, she entwined their fingers.

Sputtering from the power in his words, Sally opened and closed her mouth a few times before any sound emerged. "How dare you speak to me that way!"

"I won't tell you again." Rosco tipped his head toward her human mate. "Glenn."

"I apologize, Rosco, Leylandii. We're going." Recapturing Sally's arm, Glenn tugged her toward the front door. Sally never took her eyes off them, staring at Rosco with an expression of disbelief.

Once the door whooshed closed behind them, it was like someone pressed a button to unmute the sound of a television show. The space was flooded with chatter. Of course, Deanna caught snatches of several conversations, but her focus was on her mate. Squeezing his fingers, she was thankful for the option of using their mate link to keep their conversation private. She looked up at him.

"Are you okay?"

When he turned to look at her, his normally stormy gray eyes were brighter. Although she'd never seen his wolf, she knew those were the eyes she was seeing instead of Rosco's. Placing one hand on the side of his face, she curled her fingertips into his low beard.

"Rosco?"

"*I'm fine, Mate.*"

Cupping the hand she rested against his jaw, he tangled his fingers with hers lowering their hands from his face. Deanna wasn't convinced. His anger still pulsed low, radiating over their bond. When she quirked an eyebrow at him, he nodded and some of the heat ebbed as he let go of his annoyance.

"*Now, you're okay.*"

"*Yes, Mate. Now, I'm okay.*"

Helping her back into the booth, he slid in next to her instead of sitting on the other side. When they looked up, Mama Ley was staring at them wearing a wide smile with soft eyes.

"More fatal mates." Tapping the pad she pulled from her apron, she held up her pencil. "If the mere thought of you being mated set Sally off, she's going to completely lose her shit when she finds out it's a fatal mating. Let's not talk about when she recalls the scent of a new pup all over Deanna."

"Mama Ley..." Rosco's tone was respectful, but held an edge to it.

"That's all I have to say about it. Except for this. If she tries any mess again, I'm gonna remind her about a time in our past she thinks I've forgotten."

The promise in her statement was clear, but neither Deanna nor Rosco delved into it. Instead, they let her tell them what they wanted to eat before she bustled off to the kitchen to get their order going. Once she was gone, Rosco placed his hand over Deanna's drawing her gaze to his.

"*I'm sorry.*" Keeping their conversation private, he used their link. "*I keep having to say that, because I haven't done what I should've. I'll take care of this.*"

"*Rosco, I have a question. Did Sally ever give you any indication she wouldn't support you mating again?*"

"*No. Not that I recall.*"

"*Then, this sounds like a personal problem for her to get past. Not you, and definitely not us. You're a young wolf. Did she expect you to mourn Millie forever?*"

"*It sounds like it from the way she described how long it's been.*"

Brushing his thumb over the back of her hand, he maintained their connection. *"Either way, she needs to know her behavior was unacceptable and won't be tolerated."*

Deanna read his posture and decided to let the subject rest for the time being. However, she highly doubted it was the end of things.

~

After lunch and promises to Mama Ley not to be strangers, Deanna was once again ensconced in the passenger seat of Rosco's pickup truck, watching the scenery as they passed by. On their short trek back to where he parked, a few shifters called out greetings while others simply stared.

She gave polite smiles to the friendly and ignored the others. Having Rosco not growl at anyone else was a bonus she didn't take for granted. Apparently, the confrontation with Sally had put his protective instincts on high alert. Thankfully, the gawkers kept their opinions to themselves and didn't test the limits of his control.

As they drove past a large two-story red brick manor house, Rosco pointed it out as the Alpha house. Turning right a little ways past the Alpha house, they crossed a bridge over a small stream before Rosco pulled to a stop in front of a house very similar to the one he'd pointed out as belonging to the pack alpha.

There was already a car parked in the circular portion of the driveway. Rosco guided the truck into the attached garage and shut off the engine. By the time he came around to her side to help her from the vehicle, the occupants of the car were standing at the opening of the garage. Their smiles were a blend of anxious and eager.

Both had dark hair similar to Rosco's but only one sported the same eyes as her mate. The older woman stepped forward as Deanna and Rosco approached. The stormy gray eyes she'd passed on to her son were filled with questions. Thankfully, Rosco took the reins of the situation.

"Mama, Breena, this is my mate Deanna. Deanna, this is my mother, Eileen, and my younger sister, Breena."

Deanna gave each a nod that she hoped exuded the friendliness she was going for. It would be nice to have an amiable relationship with her mate's immediate family.

"Hello, it's very nice to meet you. Thank you so much for coming to help us with the house."

"Oh, it's no problem. I love decorating!" Slipping an arm through Deanna's, Eileen started walking toward the front of the house.

"I've secretly been wanting to do something with this place, but Rosco said—" Cutting off abruptly, Eileen's cheeks heated.

The older woman's fingers were stiff when Deanna touched them sympathetically.

"It's okay. Rosco and I talked about Millie. I'm not offended by you mentioning her name. She was and is a part of his life."

Eileen's relief was visible and audible as her shoulders dropped, and she released a sigh. Placing her other hand on top of Deanna's she squeezed her fingers.

"Thank goodness. I'm sorry my mouth ran away with me. I don't want you to think you aren't welcome simply because Rosco was mated before you."

Leaning in conspiratorially, Deanna lowered her voice—knowing everyone assembled would still hear her— "I was mated before as well. I'll have to tell you that story sometime."

Eileen beamed. "I look forward to hearing it."

Another set of fingers grasped Deanna's other arm just as they reached the front door. When she looked over, she had to look up slightly into Breena's bright face.

"It's gonna be so great having a sister again. It's just been me and mama to hold down the fort with Papa, Rosco and our three brothers."

Her statements, delivered in a soft, lyrical voice, were slightly confusing to Deanna, but she didn't dispute it. It *would* be nice to have a sister again. She hadn't spoken to her own since she left Blacktooth Summit.

From their talks, she knew Rosco also had three younger brothers. One was named Ira, who worked as a mechanic. Another, Alaric, one of the twins, was a blacksmith. The third, Roland the second of the twins, was a farmer. They hadn't encountered either of them when they went to pack town center, but Deanna didn't expect it. Rosco said Ira mainly kept to himself, Roland tended to be absorbed in his farm work and

Alaric never strayed far from his twin having his workshop located near the farm.

Rosco pushed open the front door and stood aside to let them enter first. For a place that had been closed up for goddess knows how long, the house didn't carry a prominent dank scent as Deanna would've expected. It was, however, completely empty—which she did expect. Rosco had warned her about it.

When they'd chosen not to live there, the furniture and other contents he and Millie didn't want were distributed to pack members who may have a need. From the newly mated, to essentially anyone who asked, the items had been given away. From what he told her, Rahm had done something similar with the Alpha house. In contrast, the Alpha house was currently fully furnished due to his mate Carleeta. Deanna had heard enough about the Alpha Bitch that she was eager to meet her.

Once they were done walking the downstairs with Deanna nodding to the majority of Eileen's suggestions, they went to the second level. Having just finished going through something similar with the Inn, Deanna wasn't eager to take on another such project. So, she was happy to let Eileen take the lead.

They were standing in what would be the primary bedroom once it actually contained a bed, when Deanna strolled over to the French doors leading out to a decent sized balcony. Stepping onto it, she scanned the backyard before looking across the little stream.

"Is that?..."

She wondered aloud as she stared at the back side of what she thought was the Alpha house. There were two other structures behind and to the side. Rosco stepped out beside her answering the question she didn't completely verbalize.

"Yes. It's the back of the Alpha house. Both were built almost at the same time, each having a different view of pack lands. It kept the beta close by in case of an immediate need, and vice versa."

"Oh. I guess I never thought of it that way."

"I'm guessing the set up isn't similar at Blacktooth Summit?"

"No. The beta lives near the alpha, but not within a sight line this way."

As they spoke, the back door of the house burst open. A bear and lion cub came tumbling out. They were doing the circling hopping thing younglings seemed to all do when the bear suddenly shifted into a wolf.

"What the goddess?!" Deanna leaned onto the railing, certain her eyes were deceiving her.

Rosco released a rare chuckle. "Those are Rahm and Carleeta's twins. The oldest of their growing brood. Lei-Lei is a very special cub."

"She shifted from—"

"A bear to a wolf. Give her a few seconds and she'll probably do it again. Depending on whatever game they're playing, she'll shift to the beast which gives her the best advantage."

As Rosco explained, a tall, curvy woman with glowing brown skin stepped out from one of the outer buildings, calling out to the cubs.

"There's our Alpha Bitch, Carleeta. You'll meet her soon. She asked me to come by when we leave here so she can show you some of the things she's finished that you might like."

"The things she has finished?" Again, Deanna was lost in the conversation.

"She's a carpenter, remember? She custom builds furniture suitable to a shifter's size and strength. Part of her business is in online sales, but she makes things for pack members as well."

Deanna watched Rosco as he spoke. His pride in Carleeta's accomplishments was on par with what he seemed to have in his mother and sister. Tucking that information away, she went back inside the bedroom just in time to overhear Breena and Eileen trying to whisper about the scene Sally made in the diner earlier.

The CVP grapevine worked faster than any shifter network Deanna had seen before. Since they weren't there, the only way those two could've heard about it was if someone called them before they left to meet her and Rosco at the house. The two hadn't yet noticed their presence so, Deanna limited the conversation between her and Rosco through their mating link.

"That was quicker than I thought. But it explains why they seemed kind of nervous to meet me. I thought I was supposed to be the one nervous to meet your family."

"Shifters are nosey, and gossipy. I'm sure you haven't forgotten that in your time away from pack life."

"Not entirely, but I don't recall news beating me to my own house before."

The hitch in her breath when she referred to the house as hers, caught her off guard and alerted the other two to their presence in the room. With a little jump, they sprang apart wearing guilty expressions. Rosco didn't make matters better with his gruff acknowledgement of their not-so-private conversation.

"I don't want you two giving Sally anything more to stomp around about. I'll handle it."

The set of Eileen's jaw said he was more than likely wasting his breath. Her expression was similar to the one Deanna glimpsed on Mama Ley's face before she blocked Sally's access to them.

"She's being completely unreasonable, Rosco. And if Glenn or the rest of her kin doesn't do anything about it, I don't have a problem *speaking* to her myself."

The way she said speaking, hinted to Deanna that her brand of talking might include more teeth and bite than words. Apparently, Rosco heard it as well, because he began shaking his head.

"Mama, no. I'll handle it."

"I was told she called you her son-in-law. Is it true? I know how folks like to embellish to make the gossip juicier."

Deanna slipped her hand into Rosco's when she felt the slice of hurt before he stiffened and shut it down.

"She did, Mama. But like I said. I'll handle it."

Loose brown curls with silver streaks bounced as Eileen shook her head.

"So, I guess you could only be her son if you'd spent the rest of your days pining away for Millie. Goddess forbid you be given another opportunity to be a mate and a papa."

"Mama, I really don't want to talk about Sally right now." When he looked down at Deanna, her face was turned up to his. She was certain he could see and feel her concern for him.

Chapter Eight

As appreciative as he was for his mama's concern, Rosco was getting tired of telling the matriarchs in his life to stand down from reverting to their adolescent cub and pup days. He knew both his mama and Mama Ley were formidable in their own right, but he had no desire to see them ripping Sally's little coyote apart—even if she was begging for it.

To say her response to him mating with Deanna was unexpected, was an understatement. Millie and her mother were very close. After Millie's death, Rosco continued to treat Glenn and Sally like he did his own parents. It now appeared his place in Sally's life, as her son, was always conditional.

Finally conceding to drop the subject of her tearing Sally a new asshole, his mama went back to talking about what they might need for the rest of the house. Stopping in the bedroom immediately next to the one he and Deanna would share, she and Breena stepped inside.

"This will make a great nursery. Don't you think, Mama?"

Breena smiled widely as she looked from their mother to Deanna and Rosco. He was actually surprised it took them as long as it had to mention the pup. But, considering the news of Sally's blow up had reached them so quickly, it was a given their informant told them

Deanna was pregnant. Nosey ass shifters smelled it and couldn't wait to spread the news.

However, what Rosco liked even less than someone else attempting to fight his battles, was having his mother and sister tip-toeing around him unsure if they can be excited about the new life growing in his mate's womb. He thought he'd done a better job of showing his recovery from his loss. He tossed the younglings around in play as he'd done in the past—showing that he didn't begrudge others the joy of being parents.

Their dancing around mentioning it, said his performance had fooled exactly no one. Clasping Deanna's hand in his, he tipped his head in the direction of the open doorway leading to the closet.

"If I remember correctly, there's a door in there which opens right into the room next door."

Walking through the closet revealed a built-in changing table next to a closet system obviously designed for smaller clothing. Sliding the nearly invisible pocket door, he exposed the room they'd just left on the other side.

"See."

The way his mother's eyes lit up answered whether or not she'd snooped around inside before they showed up. Deanna squeezed his fingers in approval. Even without knowing the full extent of what he'd gone through the past two summers, she wanted to assure him that she was by his side. Her responsiveness to his unspoken needs made him even more resolved to be a good mate to her. He was still very fucked up, but he didn't want any of it to touch her. Not for a second.

"This is perfect!" His mother gushed and immediately began chattering about furnishing this room for when the pups arrived.

"Pups? As in more than one?"

Deanna interrupted his mother's enthusiastic chatter. She sounded more surprised than anything, and Rosco only sensed confusion through their bond.

"Oh yes. Pups, dear. You'll likely have two, possibly three. Multiples run in the family on both sides. Rosco's father, Jonah, is a twin, as are Alaric and Roland, and I'm a triplet. It doesn't skip generations with us. These pups will be my first grand pups."

While his mama's face was alight with excitement, Deanna's lost a bit of color. The normal golden undertones of her skin seemed to suddenly wash away. In a flash, Rosco scooped her into his arms. He got no complaints from his mate as she gripped the front of his shirt with one hand while staring into his face communicating over their link.

"Did she just say she's a triplet, and your father's a twin? And you have twin brothers? Please say I heard that wrong."

When Rosco's response was delayed, she squeezed her fingers tighter gripping his shirt to the point he heard the tell-tale sound of ripping. Clasping her digits before she snatched the garment from his back, Rosco loosened her fingers.

"You heard her correctly. But, you can't take it to heart. It's just wishful thinking on her part. She's been badgering the five of us to give her grand pups for ages. Alaric, Roland and Ira aren't even mated, but it doesn't stop her from asking."

"But what if she's right?"

Lifting her slightly and nuzzling the side of her neck, Rosco responded, *"then we'll have more than one pup. We'll be okay. I'll make sure of it."*

It was as if resolving within himself to be a better mate to Deanna had released a dam blocking his feelings. Affectionate warmth flowed over their bond and he not only lapped it up, he reciprocated. The light hitch in his mate's breathing told him he'd responded correctly. The way she curved her body into his made him wish they were alone.

The light sound of someone discreetly clearing their throat punctured Rosco and Deanna's bubble. Lifting his head from where he'd buried his nose in the crook of Deanna's neck, Rosco looked up at his mother and sister. His mother's expression was soft and her eyes twinkled with a sheen of tears which she quickly dashed away.

She never said a word, but he knew she recognized the two of them using their mate link to communicate. Since his parents were one of the few fatal matings Rosco knew of prior to Rahm and Carleeta, his mother would be aware of how it worked. He had no idea of the level of intimacy he was missing by not being with his fatal mate.

"Rosco."

"Yes, Mate."

"Can you put me down please?"

Squeezing her plush curves tighter for a second, he reluctantly lowered her to her feet. The moment she wasn't pressed against him, he missed her—despite her remaining at his side. Instead of beating himself up over the feeling, he simply wrapped an arm around her waist, tugging her until their sides were glued together.

"Is everything okay?" Breena finally broke the emotionally charged silence.

"It's fine. Let's look at the rest of the rooms. I told Leeta I'd stop by so she could meet Deanna."

"Oh, well we can't keep the Alpha Bitch waiting. Her days are always full."

His mother's voice held nothing but reverence for Carleeta. Like Mama Ley, Leeta had endeared herself to most pack members. Not all, since there were females who'd desired to have her position before she and Rahm mated. Rosco made a mental note to prepare Deanna for a similar reception amongst the unmated females.

Not only had he not displayed any interest in mating again after Millie, he'd made a point of declining to mate with them with finality. For him to show up with a pregnant mate less than a summer after turning them away, would likely not go over well. Although, if they were smart, they'd keep their jealousy to themselves.

The four of them made quick work of the remainder of the tour. By the time they were done, there was a decent plan in place to tackle getting the house furnished and ready for them to move in within the next couple of weeks. As they were leaving, his mother stopped at the door of Breena's vehicle.

"Son, if you need me to, I can go to your old house and pack up your things."

Casting a knowing glance in his mother's direction, Rosco shook his head.

"It's not necessary, Mama. I'll take care of it."

There was no way he was purposely sending his mother anywhere within sniffing distance of Sally Swift. Fur would absolutely fly. Besides, he wanted to handle the situation himself to make things abundantly clear to the Swifts.

He knew Rahm would back his decision. Not only was Rosco CVP beta, he was the Greywolf family representative on the pack council. Something which had apparently slipped Sally's mind when she threw her tantrum. Rosco had the power and backing to see her kicked out of the pack.

While he didn't want things to escalate to that level, he'd do whatever it took to make certain Deanna and his pups were comfortable and safe on pack lands. He wouldn't stand for his mate to feel anything other than welcomed in her new pack home.

"Well, let me know if you change your mind. It's no bother." Try as she might, his mother couldn't hide the fire in her eyes behind her bright smile.

"I won't, but thank you for the offer." Rosco opened the door for his mother. He and Deanna watched them drive away before he lifted her into his truck to take the drive back over the creek to the Alpha house.

The short ride was silent, and they reached their next stop within a few minutes of leaving their future home. Pulling the pickup to a stop on the downside of the curved driveway, Rosco glimpsed Deanna's posture from his peripheral. The barest hint of nervousness transmitted over their link, and her hands were clasped together in her lap. Placing one hand on top of hers, he garnered her attention.

"It'll be okay. I have no doubt you and Carleeta will get along just fine. She's fair in how she treats others, the same as you."

A smile crept its way onto Deanna's face lifting the apples of her cheeks. "I hope you're right."

Squeezing her fingers, he raised her hands to his lips, kissing the backs. "I know I am."

Hopping out of the truck, he rounded the rear to get to the passenger side and opened the door for his mate. By the time she stood beside him, high pitched yips and yowls reached them followed by Carleeta's voice calling out to her children. Turning in the direction of the noise, Rosco saw Echo running full tilt in his lion cub form with Lei-Lei hot on his heels in her bear form.

Guiding Deanna away from the vehicle, Rosco stepped onto the grass in long strides crouching as he got closer to the little ones streaking in his direction. From his experience, he knew what would happen next. So, he braced himself for the moment when both furry bodies launched themselves at him. Smaller than full sized shifters, but not by any means tiny, Rosco allowed the two of them to bowl him over onto his back as they climbed on him tussling for dominance to determine who would claim the spot in the center of his chest.

"Echo, Lei-Lei. Get off of Rosco!"

Carleeta appeared above him with her hands on her hips. He was zero help getting the cubs to comply as this was the normal game they played. If the three of them were left alone, he'd likely let them scuffle until they wore themselves out, one of them conceded to the other, or they got bored and ran off.

Their mother wasn't of the same mind. When they didn't respond quickly enough to her command, she scooped them off his chest one at a time, holding their squirming bodies against her side.

"Stop that wiggling. What have I told you about throwing your little selves at folks when they come to visit?"

The cubs ceased twisting when it was obvious their mother wasn't going to let them down. Their yips became indignant chuffs.

"Who are you talking to like that?"

Carleeta looked down at her children. Heavy with her and Rahm's third child, Rosco was surprised she'd even bothered to chase the active cubs. Hopping up from the ground, Rosco lifted Echo from Carleeta's arm. He was the heavier of the two—not by much, but still heavier.

Looking over to Deanna, Rosco beckoned her forward. "Leeta, this is my mate, Deanna."

Holding out her free hand, Carleeta closed the distance between Deanna and herself.

"Hey there. Nice to finally meet you!"

A slight frown put a dip in Deanna's brow. "Finally?" She looked from Rosco to Carleeta before questioning him via their link.

"Why would she say finally?"

Shrugging, Rosco turned Echo to allow the cub to climb onto his shoulders. *"I don't know. Maybe Rahm has turned into the town crier and told her about you when I called to update him."*

Ignoring their obvious internal conversation, Carleeta half rotated

66

toward the side of the house. As if she'd heard their silent discussion, she gave Deanna a broad smile.

"Don't be too hard on Rosco. He hasn't been phoning all over CVP lands talking about you, even if he should. You're beautiful. Rahm told me about the two of you mating, but Marigold and Mama Ley have done nothing but rave about how wonderful you are, since you bought the inn."

Rosco watched the apprehension fade from his mate's posture as she moved to his side. As if she couldn't resist, she reached out to scratch between Lei-Lei's ears when the cub leaned closer sniffing at the shifter who was a stranger to her. Rosco had to act fast when Echo noticed and attempted to launch himself at Deanna to get some of the affection his sister was receiving. The action inspired laughter amongst the three adults, further relaxing his mate.

"Come on back. I have a few things I made without anyone in mind that I think you two could use."

Waving them to follow her, they walked around to the building Rahm added to hold the inventory and spare lumber for Carleeta's carpentry business. The moment they passed the back corner of the house, Carleeta's mother met them to take the cubs.

"Come on you two, shift back. It's time for you to put some clothes on. Your pop-pop will be here shortly."

"Thank you, Mama."

Carleeta handed the bear cub off with a grateful expression. Echo's little claws had to be pried off of Rosco's shirt so he walked with Milagros to the back door so he could put the little lion on his feet inside the house. When he turned back, Deanna was walking next to Carleeta nodding as the two chatted about Cummings and Deanna's pending relocation to the CVP.

Joining them at a slower pace, he gave them an opportunity for it to just be the two of them. While it wasn't mandatory for the mates of the pack alpha and beta to be friends, it helped if the two shared at least a friendly relationship. Carleeta and Millie had it. Pausing at the thought, Rosco was surprised not to feel the normal pang when he thought about his first mate. His beast was silent, but Rosco sensed the wolf's approval.

Chapter Nine

It had been a couple of days since their visit to inspect their new home and Deanna admitted to herself that it took more effort than she would've thought for her not to be overwhelmed by the welcome she received during her first trip to CVP lands. Not including the run-in with Rosco's former mother-in-law, everyone had been very receptive to their mating. She was certain once she understood pack dynamic's better, she'd be more comfortable with the eclectic group of shifters.

Born into the Blacktooth Summit pack, Deanna hadn't been in the company of such a variety of shifters before. Her pack consisted solely of wolves. Before she'd struck out on her own, she'd had very little opportunity to interact with anyone outside of other wolves. So, while she understood certain things in theory, she hadn't seen them practically applied. Such as the way shifter genetics worked.

From her previous association with Mama Ley and Marigold, Deanna knew they were a bear and wolf shifter, respectively. Mama Ley was mated to the wolf shifter who fathered both Rahm and Marigold. Rahm was a bear shifter like his mother. Marigold's mother was a human, and although Marigold had yet to shift herself, Deanna smelled the wolf in her.

It was the twins who continued to boggle her mind. Echo was a lion shifter like his mother with the same striking blue eyes, while Lei-Lei was a dual—she carried both wolf and bear equally within her. It was such a rarity only very aged shifters had ever seen it occur.

Deanna supposed she'd have plenty of time to adjust since the CVP would be her home for the foreseeable future. The more she thought on it, the more she grew to like the idea. Living as she had been, in relative isolation from other shifters, she didn't realize how much she missed the sense of community until Rosco had introduced her to his family.

Propping her feet on the ottoman in her living room, Deanna settled the laptop computer on the lap desk Rosco had provided with the device. Stating that he had to run an errand, he'd left a little while ago. It felt bizarre, bordering on unsettling, when she could no longer feel him via their bond. She didn't have to know exactly where or what he was doing to know it involved returning to CVP lands.

The past couple of days had been divided between training Hannah, and scouring the internet for furnishings after many conversations with her new mother. Yet another pleasant adjustment Deanna made as a result of her mating with Rosco. She had a mother again.

Eileen had explained that the CVP culture differed from what Deanna had grown up with. Once a couple were mated, his family became hers and vice versa. So, she wasn't a daughter-in-law. Eileen now considered Deanna her daughter, the same as Breena. Once she understood, things regarding Rosco's interaction with Sally Swift became clearer. The coyote shifter calling Rosco her son-in-law was a demotion by pack family hierarchy.

It made what she'd felt via their bond make more sense as well. At the time, there had been a layer of guilt, and something else, when Sally made her scene in the diner. Her denial of him as her son must have hurt deeply. Yet, during their tour of the Beta house, it was like a switch had flipped inside him.

Although a little rough during their actual mate bonding, he hadn't been unkind to her—his unannounced disappearance in the beginning notwithstanding—he'd been slightly withdrawn. However, when he cradled her in his arms while standing in the future nursery of their pups, there was a marked change in him. From that moment on, he became more open. Lighter in his demeanor.

Two days ago

Deanna looked at the massive bedframe in awe of Carleeta's carpentry skills. It would require a special mattress, but it would be more than adequate to handle her and a shifter of Rosco's size. Seeming to read her thoughts, Rosco stepped behind her sliding his arms around her, with his hands resting on her stomach. Without thought, she tipped her head to the side when he nuzzled her neck.

"I think this one will work." His voice was gruff even when using their mate link. "It also gives me ideas."

The word 'ideas' was accompanied by a light hip thrust allowing her to feel his thickness. Deanna wasn't sure she should be thankful or curse her above average height which allowed him better access to the rounded cheeks of her ass without contorting his body too much.

Trying to maintain her focus, Deanna stared at the sturdy bedframe with what looked like handholds carved into the headboard. The fact that her eyes went to the exact spot spoke to her not being immune to the same ideas of her lusty mate. Still, she attempted to keep her composure and ignore the way her insides clenched simply thinking of how he filled her with his thickness.

"Carleeta, are you sure this isn't meant for someone? I wouldn't want to interfere with potential profits."

Waving a dismissive hand, Carleeta shook her head. "I'm sure. I was testing out techniques with new wood when I made this one. Since more pack members have been moving back to the CVP or into the larger unoccupied homes, I knew someone could use it eventually."

"That's very kind of you." Deanna murmured only to be gently brushed off again.

Carleeta scribbled some numbers on the notepad she produced from the pocket of the apron around her expanding waist. The only commentary Rosco offered wasn't fit to be said aloud with others present. And Deanna was happy he kept it confined to their mate link.

His suggestions were wreaking havoc on her senses, making it impossible for her to remain still and causing her to rush through the remainder of the process. Mumbling nebulously about Rosco's mother and sister being in touch to coordinate more, she tried to maneuver closer to the door—only to be thwarted by the shifter who was the source of her predicament.

"What's your hurry, Kitty Kat?" Rosco practically purred the words over their mate link. "Is there something we need to rush off to take care of?"

Her joy at him confining his taunting to their mate link was diminished by the way he made certain to keep them pressed together in some capacity at all times. Deanna pasted a smile on her face as she said goodbye to Carleeta. Conversely, Rosco appeared as cool as the cucumbers growing up the trellis in the garden they passed. After teasing her with suggestions for ways to utilize their new furniture, he lingered over his goodbyes.

It was only when Carleeta's nose twitched politely that Deanna's tormentor led them from the building. Embarrassment over the scent of her need being so strong, wasn't allowed a foothold in her mind as she fled the four walls.

She was only able to give the lush garden a cursory glance as she walked back to Rosco's truck at a decidedly faster pace than she'd used when following Carleeta earlier. To add insult to horny injury, Rosco strolled behind her leisurely, as if he had nowhere pressing to be.

While technically true, the ache in her center was his fault. The aroma of her desire was strong enough to choke her. So, she knew he smelled it as well. After priming her body to be taken, he'd switched to teasing her with his delays. Ignoring her wolf's suggestions of tossing him into the grass and taking what she needed, Deanna continued to the vehicle.

Not waiting for him to open the door, she climbed in without his assistance, squirming in the seat by the time he was situated behind the wheel.

"I see my eager little Kitty Kat wants a spanking."

The strength of her arousal clouded her quick-thinking ability, so it took a beat for her to respond.

"Excuse me?"

Using one to hold the wheel as he eased them out of the driveway, his other large hand with its thick, lightly calloused fingers landed on her thigh sharing his heat through the thin barrier of her jeans.

"Who told you to open your own door?"

Deanna's frown was in genuine confusion. Staring at him, she tapped her chest with her fingertips.

"I'm capable of opening a door, Rosco."

"Just because you can, doesn't mean you should. Are you that eager for me to pound your sweet pussy?"

Deanna's breath hitched at his bluntness. Shifter's weren't known to be shy, but Rosco's boldness had dwindled after their mating heat was done. They'd coupled, but he hadn't instigated things with such direct sexual references. Her mate was either revealing another layer of himself or becoming a completely new beast right before her eyes.

Her scandalized gasp didn't stop her juices from leaking into her folds at his implication. Pounding sounded like exactly what the doctor ordered. 'Yes please', her swollen bits seemed to yell in response to his offer. The warmth from where his hand lay spread to her core, initiating a pulsing sensation. While not as demanding as when she was in heat, the throb was intense, prompting her to shift against the soft leather seats.

The movement triggered an increase in the fragrance of her arousal. It quickly filled the cab of the truck drawing a growl from her mate.

"Fuck..." The word was equally growl and groan drawing Deanna's gaze to Rosco's throat and the bobbing of the small protrusion in his neck.

Deanna had no idea where they were, and she didn't care as she sought some form of revenge against him for the way he'd revved her body earlier, leaving her aching with want. Taking the hand he used to grip her thigh, she pressed it to her aching center trapping it against her covered mons. Bridging the gap separating them, she trailed her digits along the thickness creating a bulge in his pants. The stimuli produced the desired result when Rosco hissed and his fingers curled.

The increased pressure against her slickening folds made her wish she was naked so she could luxuriate in the full effect of his rough touch. The heel of his palm held her firmly in the seat as she was suddenly jostled. Deanna's eyes jerked up to see what caused the shift in the vehicle only to realize Rosco had taken a sharp turn onto a barely visible path. Dense foliage lined either side of the makeshift road.

"Rosco?"

"This is your fault, Kitty Kat."

Her confusion was sincere as she looked from the swiftly passing land-

scape to her mate. His jaw was clenched so tightly she could see the muscle jumping near the joint. A sly smile stretched her lips as understanding took hold. Still, she played along.

"What's my fault, Wolf?"

Glaring at her from the corner of his eye, he gritted out, "we aren't going to make it to Cummings—at least not until after I fuck you."

Deanna's throaty giggle was cut off as the truck jerked to a stop between two large trees and Rosco shut off the engine.

"Don't move."

The sharp order was filled with gravel, followed by him exiting the vehicle and making it to the passenger side between two blinks. The door separating them was flung open, and Deanna was confronted with the heaving chest of her mate. His desire for her was palpable as he stared at her with such intensity it was a goddess wonder her clothes didn't melt from her body.

Before she could fully process what was happening, Rosco had spun her legs around, yanked off her pants and undies, then planted his face directly between the vee of her thighs. Tossing her head back in abandon, Deanna tilted her pelvis to offer him better access to her weeping center.

"Ahh!!"

The appreciative scream was wrenched from her throat as he attacked her clit with cruel precision sucking it into his mouth and lashing the little bundle of nerves ruthlessly. The pleasure consumed her. Nonsensical babble tumbled from Deanna's lips as her mate dined on the sweet nectar dripping from her core. In a ridiculously short amount of time Rosco took her to the precipice of release and callously tossed her into the abyss.

His satisfied growls were muffled against her pussy once her thick thighs clamped tightly around his head while she was in the throes of orgasm. Rosco did nothing to maintain his ability to breathe. Instead, he redoubled his efforts sending her crashing into a second release on the heels of her first.

When she could do nothing but slump limply in the seat, he pushed her legs apart, lined his thickness up to the opening of her slick tunnel and slid home, filling her completely. Closing her eyes, Deanna rocked into his questing thrusts. It was absolute bliss.

From the slight bite of pain in the way he stretched her walls, to the tight grip he had on her thighs, to the way he jerked her into his every stroke—absolute bliss.

"That's it, Kitty Kat. Take me. Take all of me inside your tight pussy. Squeeze my cock and drain me dry."

Through half lowered lashes, Deanna observed Rosco as he watched the place where they were joined together. His stormy gray eyes appeared more silver than gray and his nose flared with each punch forward of his hips. His dark hair flopped onto his forehead as he exerted himself. Rosco's cock was so deep inside her Deanna swore he was trying to tunnel his way to her chest. And she didn't care. Coupling with him inspired feelings she couldn't begin to articulate with a clear head, let alone when he was feeding her his thick shaft, robbing her of coherent thought.

Her next orgasm caught her completely unawares, snatching her voice so that she could only emit a silent scream as her mate did exactly as he promised and pounded her pussy. His grunts joined her moans as he pummeled her flower until he came to a stuttering stop. His seed had already found a home in her womb, but it didn't stop him from pumping it into her grasping channel.

Present

Deanna was jerked back into the present by the quiet snick of the door closing. Looking up, she turned her unseeing gaze from the laptop screen to the shifter standing just inside the room. Tilting his head to one side, a corner of Rosco's lips tipped up into a smirk.

"It doesn't smell like you've been ordering furniture. Unless, of course spending money makes your pussy wet."

Not giving Deanna a chance to answer, he closed the distance between them in long strides and rotated the laptop to see the website for custom mattresses on the screen. His quick glimpse of the display turned his smirk into a full-fledged smile.

"Oh... I see what's going on. Don't worry, Kitty Kat. I'll help you clear your head so you can focus."

Moving the computer and lap desk safely away, he tugged her down on the sofa blanketing her body with his. Any words of protest Deanna may have had were swallowed in the kiss Rosco placed on her lips. It was quite some time later before she thought of anything beyond losing herself in her mate.

Chapter Ten

Rosco rolled to a stop in front of the closed garage door. The home he'd left a little over two weeks ago appeared so different, although nothing about the place had changed in the time he was away. No. He was the change. The previous weight of his loss didn't feel as heavy, and the guilt associated with being bonded to his fatal mate didn't cut as deeply.

There were still items that lingered. One doesn't get over such a thing by simply saying it's done—time to move on. If only it worked so easily. Leaving the truck, he manually opened the garage door. Glenn had offered more than a few times to install an automatic opener, but Rosco declined. He wasn't a fan of too many electronic devices. Some things he'd become accustomed to tuning out, but he liked to keep them to a minimum around his home.

Before he drove the rest of the way inside, he cast a glance to the left toward the Swift's home. No one was outside, but it didn't mean no one was there. When he left the inn, he'd told Deanna he had a few errands to run. He'd waited until a couple of the security team were posted nearby prior to leaving. There was no visible threat, no hint of one, but Rosco wouldn't leave Deanna unprotected—especially not when he wasn't within communication range for their link.

Despite it being only days since he'd mated with Deanna, not hearing her voice in his head or sensing her emotions vibrating over their bond felt so foreign he nearly turned around to bring her with him. But, he knew this was something he needed to do alone. Unless she wanted to see it, he didn't intend to ever bring her to this house.

The place was filled wall to wall with memories of his life with Millie. Rosco determined it was unfair to expect Deanna to be comfortable in such a place. She'd expressed her desire for him not to pretend he wasn't mated previously, and she didn't want him to forget his first mate. But, it simply felt...wrong...to Rosco to place her in that position. Especially since the Swifts lived right next door.

Confronting Sally was one of the 'errands' on Rosco's list. For a brief moment he considered the wisdom of not allowing his mother to step in. While he didn't need his mommy to fight his battles, it wouldn't bode well for the pack beta to appear as if he was abusing an older pack female. That thought aside, he needed it to be abundantly clear to Sally how he expected Deanna to be treated.

He wouldn't tolerate any maligning of his mate by anyone, not even the woman he'd considered his second mother for a large chunk of his adult life. She would not be immune from his wrath if Deanna came to harm, be it physical or emotional.

Once he stepped over the threshold into the house, the barrage of emotions he anticipated didn't materialize. He'd put off coming to pack up his things and mentally flip-flopped on allowing his mother and Breena to do it for him. However, he needed to do it on his own. He had to prove, if only to himself, that he was fully committing to Deanna— not simply yielding to the dictates of the goddess.

While he and Millie weren't big travelers, there were pieces of luggage which made it easy to pack his clothing as well as some of his personal items. Not having an abundance or excess of either of those meant he made short work of emptying the closet and drawers.

Once his bags were packed and sitting next to the bedroom door, Rosco paused to look around the room. The bed still looked like he or Millie could walk in at any moment and slide beneath the covers. The quilt her grandmother gifted them when they had their official wedding was still folded down across the bottom. Staring at it made him remember an item he did want to take with him.

Crossing the hall, Rosco steeled himself before he pushed open the door to a mostly empty room. The original plan for the space was to make it into a nursery. The other two rooms were used for the rare guest and would be converted once their pups were old enough to move out of the nursery. Those days would never come. At least not for him and Millie.

Rosco would have them with Deanna. And, he was sincerely beginning to look forward to the possibility more each day. There was no bed, crib or cradle in the room. Only a dresser with a built-in changing table and a rocking chair remained inside. He and Deanna wouldn't need the dresser, but the rocking chair was a gift from his father. So, Rosco moved it into the hallway to take with him to the Beta house.

When he turned back, he walked over to the changing table, but didn't see what he was looking for. Pulling open the drawers, he was met each time with disappointment. There was no reason it shouldn't be there. He'd been in this room less than a month ago and it was laying on top of the changing area.

Even knowing it was unlikely he'd moved it and forgotten, he searched the room and the closet before returning to give his bedroom the same treatment. In his heart of hearts, Rosco knew exactly what had happened. He'd brushed off the light lingering scent when he'd entered the house because he'd had visitors prior to taking his forced vacation. But, no he had to face it. One of the Swifts or Carnahans had been there while he was away.

Stalking through the house, he exited the door closest to their property. His long legs ate up the distance, and he was standing on their front porch in seconds. Extending them a courtesy he hadn't been given, he delivered firm knocks against the door frame.

The door swung open. Glenn's face was initially stretched into a smile, but it quickly melted away when he saw the fury in Rosco's expression. Rosco made no attempt to hide or tamp down his anger.

"What's wrong?" Glenn stepped back, opening the door wider, inviting Rosco inside.

"Where's your wife?" Rosco had zero politeness left in him at the moment. Sally had severely overstepped.

"She's upstairs. Rosco, what's wrong?" Glenn's brow knitted in obvious concern. Rosco just wasn't certain if the concern was reserved for him or Sally.

"Call her down. She has some explaining to do."

Glenn finally caught on to Rosco's stance and went to the bottom of the stairs to call for his wife. With her enhanced shifter hearing, Rosco was certain she'd heard him when the door opened, but she'd waited for her husband to actually call her name before her footfalls were heard moving across the floor above.

Her steps were deliberate and slow. Glenn glanced at Rosco when it was taking longer than strictly necessary for her to appear.

"I'll just go up and get her."

Mutely nodding, Rosco worked to quiet his beast's internal grumbling. Like him, his wolf wasn't just offended at Sally's overstepping. He was angry that she would dare steal from them. Theft wasn't common in shifter communities. They didn't bother to lock their doors because it was so rare. Who bothers to steal when their scent immediately gives away their presence wherever they've been? Only the brazen. And those who'd not been confronted with the consequences of their actions.

Tuning his ear to the conversation between his former in-laws, Rosco tilted his head to the side as one corner of his mouth kicked up. Glenn was giving Sally hell. Not one ounce of sympathy could be drummed up when the usually soft-spoken man's voice grew gruff as he spoke to his wife.

"Sally, what the hell did you do? Why is Rosco in our living room looking like he's ready to wolf out at any second?"

"Keep your voice down, Glenn. I didn't do anything. Just like you told me the other day, I'm leaving him and his new whore alone."

"Stop it, Sally! I mean it. I won't stand for you talking about Rosco's mate that way. You don't know her and have no reason to believe the lies you're spewing. I don't even recognize you right now. But, what I do know is this, you're gonna take your ass downstairs and make whatever you did right."

Virtual silence followed Glenn's directive. All Rosco could detect was the sounds of their breathing. It was likely a standoff between them. Despite Glenn being human, he'd held his ground on more than one occasion with shifters. Living in a community where some children were physically stronger than him could be humbling. However, Glenn had done it for over thirty summers.

It was actually less than a minute following Glenn's demand that Sally's feet once again began to move. By the time she was halfway down the stairs, Rosco knew she wasn't going to comply with her husband's mandate. Her hands were empty.

"Where is it, Sally?" Rosco didn't allow her to make it all the way down the stairs.

"I don't know what you're talking about, Rosco Greywolf. Where is what?"

"Sally, I'm not stupid and neither are you. We both know you were in my house. Recently. And you took something I would've never given you. Now, where is it?"

Redness crept up Sally's neck settling in her cheeks. The banister she gripped creaked under the pressure. Her lips were pinched to the point of disappearing into her face. Glenn stopped on the step next to her looking between Rosco and Sally. It was obvious to Rosco, Glenn was completely lost to what his wife had done.

"Where is what? What is he talking about, Sally?"

When she said nothing, a growl rumbled from Rosco's chest. "You have this one chance to hand it over. If I have to sniff it out, I'll rip this place down to the studs."

His promise was what broke Sally's cone of silence. "Don't be ridiculous, Rosco. You'd tear up our home over a blanket?"

The shifter before him was a completely different creature from the one who'd smiled at him over dinner less than a month ago—at the table not twenty feet from where they currently stood. None of their recent past seemed to matter to her. So, Rosco wouldn't allow it to affect him either.

"It's not just a blanket and you know it. It was the one Millie and my mother made together. Now, this is your last chance to do this the decent way. Give. Me. The. Blanket."

The rumble in Rosco's chest increased in volume announcing his wolf was very close to the surface. Sally's eyes widened giving her first emotion other than anger in the slight movement.

"There's no need for that, Rosco." Turning on his wife, he hissed, "I can't believe you, Sally! What in the world has gotten into you? I should've known you and Eugenia were up to something when you had your heads together yesterday."

Not waiting for an answer, he stomped back up the stairs. "I know where it is, son. I'll get it for you."

"No, you won't, Glenn! My daughter made it with her hands for *her* pup. Not for him and that—"

"Say it, Sally. Say it and you'll wish you weren't able to release sound ever again."

Sally jumped a foot at the nearness of Rosco's gruff voice to her ear. When she realized how close he was to her, she clamped her lips closed and eased backwards up the stairs. Rosco followed matching each backward step with one of his own.

If his facial expression matched the emotions churning in his gut, he looked ready to wreak havoc. Because he was. With zero compunction. By the time Sally had inched her way backwards up the staircase, Glenn was standing on the landing holding the soft yellow knit blanket with silver embroidery along the edge spelling out *Greywolf*.

Reaching above Sally's head, Glenn passed him the baby blanket. Mutiny was etched into Sally's features but she remained quiet. It was the smartest thing she'd done in many days. Shooting his wife a glare as he strode past her, Glenn stopped next to Rosco on the stair.

"Son, I don't know what's gotten into her. And I won't apologize on her behalf. That's for her to do. I will apologize for not recognizing what was going on and putting a stop to it. It should've never gotten this far."

Offering Glenn the barest of nods in acknowledgement, Rosco turned to descend the stairs. Stopping at the bottom, he rotated to make certain they were both in his line of sight again.

"I will only say this once. So, let me be clear. You will *not* speak *to* or *of* my mate in a negative way. If you don't think you can manage to be civil, stay the fuck away from us. There will be consequences for going against me on this. I will *not* stand for my mate to feel unwelcome in her new home."

Having said his piece, Rosco issued another harsh glare before turning on his heel to leave. Glenn didn't follow him and as Rosco slammed the door behind him, he heard the beginnings of the Swift's argument. Rosco didn't pause or break stride as sounds of their dispute faded the farther away he got. They were still at it when he backed his truck out into the driveway and let the garage door down.

Heading to his next destination, he first stopped at the alpha's office at pack town center. He needed to get Rahm up to speed as to what was going on and line someone up to clear everything out of that house. He wouldn't take it to the Beta house with him, but it wouldn't be left there for Sally and her sister, Eugenia, to pick over.

When he walked inside the office, Rahm was there. Casting his gaze about, Rosco looked for the shifters his nose told him should be there.

"Hey, Rosco. I didn't expect to see you today. I thought you were busy with your mate trying to get things set up across the creek."

Dropping heavily into the leather chair opposite Rahm's desk, Rosco scrubbed a hand through his hair.

"Yeah, I was. I am. I stopped by my place to get my shit and had a run in with Sally."

Leaning back in his chair, Rahm quirked an eyebrow. "What the fuck did Sally do this time? Mama told me about the stunt she pulled in the diner. Am I gonna regret telling my mama she couldn't go over there and beat her ass?"

Rosco nodded as he replied, "probably just as much as I regret telling my mama the same thing."

Quickly filling Rahm in on what had just occurred and the malice in the interaction with the Swifts—Sally in particular. He didn't leave out Glenn's assumption that Eugenia Carnahan was involved. It tracked with the scents Rosco picked up when he'd entered the ranch style home he once shared with his deceased mate.

"I won't have Deanna feeling unwelcome here, Rahm. Despite what you saw that morning a few days ago. I care about my mate. She's amazing, and I don't deserve her. But she's mine. No one. And I do mean **no one** is going to talk shit to or about her without consequences."

Clasping his hands on the desk in front of him, Rahm pierced Rosco with a knowing stare. "I think I know where this is going, but you're gonna have to make it plain."

"I want to officially put her on notice. With the council."

"Are you sure?" Rahm tapped his fingertips against the desk.

"Yes. I don't know what's going on with her and I don't care. What I do know is I won't have my mate upset and uncertain about her reception here—especially not with my pup growing inside her."

Rosco didn't have to say it aloud. He'd already lost one mate and pup due to someone else's callous actions. He wasn't going to allow any harm, no matter how small, to come to Deanna. It was untenable.

Nodding, Rahm met his gaze with unspoken understanding. "Unless you want to call a special meeting, the next one is scheduled for three days from now."

"I can wait. We should have everything we need to move in by then. That'll work."

"You'll want to get in touch with Shep. He's stationed out of Georgia now, with a special team like the one Brody was on—but without the homicidal commanding officer. As the Swift family representative on the council, he should be made aware of what's happening in his family."

While he hadn't completely forgotten about Millie's younger brother, it hadn't occurred to Rosco to contact Shep about his mother's behavior. It was highly probable he wouldn't get him on the phone, but Rosco made a mental note to at least give it a try before the end of the day.

Spending the next few moments catching up on other pack happenings, Rosco solicited Rahm's help in getting a few of the younger shifters to go to his old place and finish packing it up. With the exception of the quilt, which would be given to his mother, the items were to be stored with the other things Carleeta kept on hand for newly mated and young pack members striking out on their own.

Once those plans were made, Rosco left the office anxious to get his other obligations completed so he could get back to his Kitty Kat. They'd been separated longer than he'd planned.

Chapter Eleven

Deanna took one final look around the bedroom she'd called home for more a year. It had felt good to put roots down and have something to call her own again. Technically, she still owned the Inn. She wasn't selling it, just turning over much of the day to day to Hannah and Mrs. Kimble. The older woman had been a goddess send when she answered the posting Deanna placed on the Cummings community message board.

The retired bookkeeper was happy to transition to helping Hannah take care of the Inn with Deanna relocating to CVP lands. The change of address didn't mean Deanna wouldn't be involved—just not so hands on. Things had changed. Quickly.

Touching her stomach, Deanna marveled at the turn her life had taken. She'd spent much of her adult existence thinking she wasn't meant to be a mother. It had been a difficult situation to acknowledge. But once she did, she resolved to be happy with the other ways she was blessed by the goddess. After getting away from Barry and the disdain of her family, Deanna blossomed.

She had no idea when she'd begun browsing the small-town real estate listings that she would pick a place so close to the home of her fatal mate—a shifter she hadn't believed existed until she met him. As her thoughts turned to her mate, Rosco strolled into the room.

"Did we miss something, Kitty Kat?"

Glancing over her shoulder, Deanna shook her head. "No. Just giving the place one last look over."

Enveloped by warmth when Rosco slid his arms around her, holding her body close to his, Deanna sighed at how good it felt. Despite their rough beginning, Rosco was an attentive mate. Generous with his affections. A far cry from what she'd experienced during her first mating.

"Well, I have the truck loaded, Robeson is going to drive your car."

"I'm perfectly capable of driving my own car, Rosco."

Tightening his hold marginally, Rosco nuzzled the side of her neck. "I'm aware, but you're still riding with me."

Deanna realized arguing with him was pointless. And it wasn't like she minded being driven around. She simply wasn't keen on completely giving up her hard-earned independence. Her new mate was very protective of her, even with small things.

With another kiss to the exposed skin of her neck, Rosco gave a rubbing pat to her stomach before setting her away from him.

"If you're all done, it's time to go, Kitty Kat."

Nodding, Deanna laced her fingers with his and allowed him to lead her from the room, through the lobby and out of the building. Along with the decision not to argue with him, she'd given up on explaining to him that she was a wolf as well—which meant his new nickname for her didn't quite fit.

He brushed her off, reminding her of her own middle name before displaying the ways she practically purred under his touch. Although a formal demonstration wasn't necessary, Deanna didn't try to dissuade him from doing so.

The sun was bright in the sky making her wish for a hat or something to shield her eyes other than the hand she placed above them to semi block the glare as she glanced around at the nearly deserted Main street. Her gaze faltered when she saw something in the distance near the hardware store.

Well...not something. More like someone. Blinking hard, she

scrubbed her hand over her eyes and looked again. There was no one propped against the pickup truck in front of the store.

"*Is something wrong, Mate?*" Rosco's concern coated the words delivered via their link and pulsed through their bond.

"*I'm fine. My eyes are playing tricks on me. I thought I saw someone I knew down there near the hardware store.*"

Looking in the direction of the establishment, Rosco narrowed his eyes and tilted his head back. Deanna was certain he was attempting to catch a scent. Inhaling deeply, the only scent prevalent to her was Rosco's, which eased her mind. Her eyes may have been playing tricks on her, but her nose didn't lie.

After a brief moment, Rosco assisted her into the vehicle and buckled her safety belt. He didn't acknowledge what he did or didn't detect. Rounding the car once he handed her inside, he kept his gaze trained on the hardware store. Deanna had nearly forgotten about Robeson until Rosco lifted two fingers to his own eyes then pointed toward Robeson and the hardware store. His message was clear. *Keep an eye on that place.*

She wouldn't question his instincts. Her mate was showing himself to be an affable shifter, but his prowess was unmistakable. In his humanoid form he was large—even for a shifter. They'd gone on a run allowing their wolves to meet, and his wolf was almost twice the size of hers. Large, silvery grey and beautiful. His beast inspired confidence in his ability to defend and protect.

Simply knowing Rosco was watching over her was enough to ease Deanna's mind, regardless of if she thought there was a real cause for concern or not. The truck dipped and rocked slightly when he dropped his weight into the driver's seat.

The ride to their new home was pretty uneventful. Now familiar with the landscape, seeing it held more comfort than the anxiety she felt during her first visit to the CVP. Now, less than two weeks later, she was taking up permanent residence.

A smile brightened Deanna's expression once she saw the cars parked in the circular drive at the front of the Beta house. The mothers were already here, along with Breena and Carleeta. Rosco's mother, who insisted Deanna call her *mama* and Mama Ley were already there. They must have only just arrived, because they stood on the extended front porch instead of being inside the house.

Once Rosco stopped the truck just outside of the garage, Deanna was nearly dancing in her seat. Having them there to greet her sent a familial warmth coursing through Deanna. It was a feeling she hadn't experienced in quite some time. If ever.

Robeson drove her smaller SUV into the space on their left and two other vehicles pulled into the circular drive. Deanna was slightly confused as most of their things had already been delivered. She wasn't sure what the need was for the additional hands. Shrugging, she chalked it up to a CVP thing.

By then, Rosco was at her door to help her out and she was swept into the activities with the ladies and the others who'd arrived to lend a hand or say hello. She finally got the opportunity to meet Rosco's three younger brothers, as they were all there to help. She'd met his father on a previous occasion.

Their new home was buzzing with activities for the next few hours. Deanna came close to pouting when she realized she was only allowed to point and direct. She couldn't so much as lift the lid on a box without Rosco or someone else being there to pick it up or ask her where she wanted the items inside placed.

Their kindness bordered on overwhelming. It wasn't as if her life with the Blacktooth Summit Pack was entirely unhappy, but they didn't often have new shifters join the pack. So, the rallying of the community to make a body feel welcome wasn't something Deanna had much experience with.

She was still adjusting to the differences in the pack make up in comparison to the homogeneity of Blacktooth. The CVP had shifters ranging from fauns to bears to cougars, lions and wolves. That they all existed, relatively peacefully, was astounding. Seeing the way they intermarried and truly considered one another family was a study of which she would probably never tire.

By the time they showed the last of their welcome home committee to the door, every piece of furniture had been uncovered, assembled where necessary, and placed into the respective rooms based on Deanna's preferences. The kitchen items had been unpacked and put away, and a veritable buffet had been laid out for everyone who stopped by, whether they helped or not. Before they left, the space was put back to order so neatly only the lingering aroma of the savory meal indicated anything had ever occurred.

Her belly was pleasantly filled as Deanna stood in front of the triple sink vanity staring at her reflection in the mirror. As she sectioned her hair to plait it before tying it down, she really looked at herself for the first time in a while. She stood by her growth after striking out on her own, but there was a new light in her eyes. One she didn't recall ever seeing.

That was saying something, because in the beginning of her first mating, Deanna sincerely believed she was happy. Until she wasn't. But now, she knew there could've never been the depth between them like she'd experienced in far less time with Rosco. Simply watching him interact with the shifters who came to the house held her enthralled.

Little by little, her mate's layers were being peeled away. He had a sarcastic, and more than a little wry, sense of humor which resulted in snappy comebacks to things the members of pack security said to him— whether in jest or not. She was now accustomed to the gruffness of his voice and knew it wasn't an indicator of his displeasure, but simply the way he spoke.

The timbre rarely failed to send a shiver down her spine to settle into unseen regions of her body. More than once that day she'd been forced to relocate to keep from spraying the scent of her desire all over the room. Shifters being shifters, no one would've batted an eye, but there was no point in wasting all the help their welcoming committee offered.

Just as she pinned the last plait to her head, Rosco entered the bathroom. Continuing with her task of tying on her colorful headwrap, Deanna didn't visibly react when he stopped behind her, resting his hands on the countertop on either side of her hips. The heavy weight of his cock rested against her covered ass telegraphed his nudity. Once she was done knotting the material, he leaned closer, resting his chin on her shoulder.

Catching his gray gaze in the reflective glass, Deanna reached up to run her fingers through his short strands. In the brief time since they'd met, his hair had grown out slightly. Although she hadn't asked him not to cut it, she admitted to enjoying the additional length.

When Rosco's dexterous digits tugged at the knot keeping her robe closed, Deanna's fingers tightened in his silky strands. The scent of her arousal hit the air a moment later drawing a growl from her amorous mate.

"Mmm...Kitty Kat. Do I smell what I think I smell?"

Not giving her a chance to answer, in the span of a breath, Rosco had her robe open delving into her folds, zeroing in on her clit. His efforts were immediately rewarded with the sweet aroma of her juices leaking from her channel.

"Yeah...That's exactly what I thought."

Seeming to talk mostly to himself, Deanna gasped when she was suddenly whipped around. With her bare ass quickly planted on the cool granite surface, her mate dropped to his knees before her, tossed her legs onto his shoulders and dove face first into her pulsing center.

Finding his hair again, this time with both hands, Deanna held on as Rosco pleasured her pussy so thoroughly with his mouth, causing her to crest into her first screaming orgasm only moments later. She could safely say it was her first of the night because it was rare for her mate to deliver just one trip to paradise. They normally came in twos and threes.

"Fuck."

The word was growled against her mons, as her mate lapped at the essence still trickling from her grasping walls. His tongue brushed against her folds stimulating her clit. The sensation of him seeking to devour each drop was prevalent.

"Umm...Rosco...Please..."

The moaned request pushed past Deanna's lips as she squirmed against the smooth surface of the vanity. The heat radiating from her core was consuming her body and she had to have him inside her. Immediately.

"I've got what you need, Kitty Kat. No begging required."

With one final kiss to her swollen pussy lips, he lowered her legs until they rested in the crook of his arms. Grasping her hips in his big hands he pulled her toward him as he pushed his hips forward burying his thickness inside her. The arch in her back thrust Deanna's breast into the air while her head rocked backwards on her shoulders, tearing her mouth away from his kiss.

"So deep…" The words dropped from her lips unbidden as Rosco swiveled his hips on the next stroke into her honeyed walls.

Deanna felt her pussy trying to grip and hold him inside, as he tunneled in and out of her greedy channel. Her fingers curled against his forearms where her nails were likely to leave divots that would heal before morning. Rosco didn't acknowledge the pain, if there was any. So, Deanna held on for dear life as her mate pummeled her channel exactly the way she liked, taking her to the edge of bliss and tossing her pussy first into a toe-curling release.

His grunts and growls joined her moans and sighs as he emptied himself inside her, coating her womb with his seed. In the aftermath, his hips jerked, and his hold on her remained firm as he kept his cock buried inside her while they came down from their orgasmic high.

Capturing her lips in a kiss that felt like he was far from done with her, Rosco confirmed Deanna's thoughts by lifting her from the counter. Still empaled on his turgid length, she wrapped her legs around him as he walked them into the enormous shower.

The space was definitely constructed with shifters in mind. And she and her mate took advantage of the additional room. They fucked all over that shower rendering the work Deanna had done to tame her hair useless. As her walls clamped around Rosco's hard cock, she couldn't bring herself to care. Finally sated, she slumped against his chest after riding him to their fourth, or was it fifth, orgasm? Either way, sleep was the friend calling to her as she lay cradled in her mate's arms.

She vaguely recalled Rosco tending to her before wrapping her hair in a towel and putting her to bed. When his warmth once again enveloped her body, she was tugged under fully into dreamland.

Chapter Twelve

Rosco glanced out of the window for what was likely the twentieth time in as many minutes. Today was his first official day getting back into his duties as beta. It was also the day of the council meeting. He wasn't worried about the meeting. He was anxious because Deanna was wandering around pack lands without him.

Of course, she was with his sister, but she wasn't with *him*. It felt wrong. He didn't know why, but it did. The feeling wouldn't let up. A rush of warmth and calm reached him over their mate bond as Deanna shared her feelings with him. The sensation preceded her voice in his head.

I'm fine, Big Bad. You can stop worrying. At this moment, I'm sitting in a comfortable chair talking to Miss Milagros, while we watch the cubs play in the grass

He appreciated the update, he really did, however the mental image conjured by her explanation of her activities drew his brow into a frown. Those chairs weren't situated close to any trees or shaded area. The days were cooler, but the sun was still blazing high in the sky.

"It's pretty hot today. Don't forget to drink water and maybe find a shadier place to sit."

Couching it as a suggestion was the best he could do, when he really wanted to order her to the shade or inside the house for that matter. But he knew he couldn't. His mate was an agreeable shifter, but she'd only let him boss her so much. Which suited him just fine. He enjoyed the push and pull before he finally got her to concede. Her concessions were the best part.

A smile tipped up the corners of his lips as he thought back to the previous night. He'd known Deanna's desire had been at a low hum all day. How he'd had the restraint not to take her into one of the vacant rooms and sink inside her, he didn't know. It was a miracle within itself. She wanted to do more to help with the unpacking, and he didn't want her over exerting herself.

He'd won, but it had been thoroughly entertaining to watch her snap her mouth closed each time an item was lifted from her fingers. If he'd been certain he wouldn't toss her over his shoulder, he would've kissed away the pout she sported afterwards. But a shifter had to know his limits. Putting his lips on his beautiful mate was a pathway to fuckville. Not that he didn't fully enjoy every visit to that magical place, but they were in the midst of putting their house in order at the time.

"You ready for today?" Rahm cut into Rosco's lascivious reminiscence, jerking him back into the moment.

"Ready as I'm going to get."

Rosco didn't relish the thought of calling Sally to task in front of the council, but it needed to be done. When he'd spoken to Shep, his packmate was understanding. Like his father, he couldn't believe his mother's behavior. It was very much a far cry from the sweet person Shep had known, and he said as much.

While he was away on military assignment, his father stepped back in as the Swift family representative on the pack council, but everyone knew Glenn's heart wasn't in the role and he'd pretty much gone along with what Sally wanted. Rosco wasn't looking forward to the potential outcome of the day.

However, Sally hadn't let up. Despite his warnings to keep her opinions of Deanna to herself, she'd continued to spread her discontent. Of course, it had gotten back to him. Only knowing what Rosco planned had kept his and Rahm's mothers from going to the Swifts to have a *little chat,* as they called it, with Sally.

Leaving the smaller building housing the pack alpha and beta offices, Rosco walked beside Rahm to the larger structure where council meetings were held. Neither of them spoke. It wasn't necessary. Rahm knew where Rosco stood. He'd admitted Rosco had responded much better than him, renewing his offer to give Sally an ultimatum if she wanted to remain with the CVP.

Rosco didn't take him up on the offer. No matter how tempting. They'd do this by pack tradition. His grievances would be aired in public—not skulking around in secret in the manner Sally had resorted to using.

Other shifters were arriving as well. Some glanced at Rosco with sympathy laden expressions, but he didn't miss a few of the pinched faces. He was happy Deanna wouldn't be anywhere near the activities about to occur. To make certain she wasn't touched by any of it, he'd put up a mental barricade to prevent his anger from filtering through to her.

Although she would expect something, because she was aware of his plans. As his mate, Rosco didn't consider Deanna an outsider. But, he knew she still viewed herself as one, as did some members of the pack. He allowed it to work in his favor, since she wasn't aware that all CVP members were allowed to attend pack council meetings.

They weren't allowed a vote, unless they represented their family in the assembly, but they could attend to hear and voice their opinion on the happenings in the pack. It appeared today was one of the days other pack members decided to exercise their right—including his mother. Now he understood why only Breena was with Deanna.

Alongside her, was her partner in crime, Mama Ley. Both wore pleasant expressions. Rosco wasn't fooled by their calm demeanor.

"Do you see what I see?" Issuing the words at a barely detectible whisper, Rosco glanced at Rahm.

"Yep. Personally, I say let 'em take turns kicking her ass. She's begging for it."

Rosco was torn between agreeing with Rahm and acknowledging

that Sally was acting out because she was in pain. It didn't excuse her behavior toward him. It especially didn't make it right for her to run her mouth about his mate. Deanna hadn't done a thing to Sally—except exist.

As everyone filed into the meeting room, Rosco took his seat to Rahm's right. His location was indicative of his position as the pack beta. However, he was one of the only pack members who carried two votes on the council. He had one as beta, and he was also the Greywolf family representative.

The council had less than twenty voting members with families rotating on and off in a predetermined cycle. So, for the next five summers, he would serve in a dual capacity.

The struggle to keep his wolf under control began the second the beast scented Sally, announcing the appearance of the Swifts. Glenn was present along with their youngest son, Silas. Barely out of his teens, the young coyote stared wide eyed at the assembly. It was obvious he'd never been inside the hall, let alone attended a council meeting.

A few minutes later, Rahm rapped his knuckles against the hardwood table. There was no gavel like Rosco had heard the humans used. The sound was loud enough to carry to every shifter and human ear in the room.

"Okay, let's get this meeting started. We have a few things on the agenda, and I'm sure no one wants to be here any longer than we have to be."

Trust Rahm to cut through the bullshit and set the tone for having an expeditious meeting. Rosco was certain Rahm didn't expect it to be absent theatrics, which was probably why he started with the small items saving Rosco's petition for last.

"And now we move to the final item on the agenda." Rahm looked up from the papers in front of him, eyeing Rosco.

"Rosco." His name was the only prompt Rahm gave him to let him know it was his turn.

Leaning forward, Rosco rested his forearms on the table. He panned his gaze around the room before coming to a rest on Sally. Her face was pinched disapprovingly—and he'd yet to say anything. His wolf paced in the galley of his mind. Contained. For the moment.

"As many of you know, I recently mated again. Deanna owns the Inn located in Cummings."

Murmurs of congratulation came from more than a few shifters around the room. From his periphery, he noticed, his and Rahm's mothers sitting up straighter, with their arms folded. They were staring directly at Sally as everyone waited for Rosco's next words.

Normally, he wasn't prone to theatrics, or being overly loquacious, but something drove him to be more open than usual.

"I appreciate your well wishes, but it appears not everyone is happy the goddess blessed me with another mate."

Allowing his gaze to settle on Sally, he continued. "As more than one person is here, who was present in the diner the first day I brought my new mate to pack lands, you are aware Sally Swift spoke ill of my mate and she continued to do so after that day."

"I did not!" Sally's outburst was immediately quieted by her husband.

"Sally!" The authority in Glenn's voice belied his normal genial manner.

Hugging herself, Sally fumed in her seat—staring at Rosco defiantly.

"We are a free pack, and each shifter is entitled to their feelings and opinions. However, we have long done away with tolerating divisiveness amongst us. Sally Swift's behavior goes against pack cohesiveness. In addition to spreading unfounded rumors about my mate, she entered my home and stole something dear to me."

A collective gasp swept through the room. It didn't matter how small the item. Stealing wasn't tolerated in their community. Not when they shared amongst their pack freely.

"I didn't steal it! It was my daughters! I can't believe you brought me before the council over a measly blanket."

Venom dripped from each word Sally spoke. Her cheeks reddened, and her breaths came in heaving puffs.

Despite not having permission, Rosco's mother spoke up.

"If the blanket was so measly, why did you want it so badly?"

"Mom." Rosco didn't look at his mother. He kept his gaze firmly on

Sally. He wanted there to be no mistaking anything he said or did. Muttering under her breath, his mother quieted.

"You know the rules, Sally. Theft isn't tolerated here. Nor is intentionally seeking to disrupt pack cohesion."

Disregarding her husband's censuring stare, Sally sprang up from her seat.

"Don't you dare sit there passing judgment on me, Rosco Greywolf! You're galivanting all over CVP and Cummings with that woman as if my daughter meant nothing.

So what if I wanted a piece of her and my first grandchild with me. It's my right! You're trying to give that trollop my Millie's life!"

Even if he'd wanted to contain his beast, Rosco would've been unable to hold himself in check. The leap from his seated position into the small space between the rows of chairs where the Swifts were seated occurred so quickly, not even Rahm was able to stop him.

"What did I tell you about speaking ill of my mate?" A growl infiltrated his words. Shooting a glare at Glenn who shoved Sally behind him while Silas stood looking bewildered and conflicted about what he should do, Rosco stared at her. Rosco eclipsed the males in height, weight and strength. He could easily take on both. But his fight wasn't with them. And was unlikely to get physical no matter how much his beast clawed to get out.

Looking over Glenn's shoulder, Rosco continued to glare at Sally, who stared back defiantly.

"You *will* keep my mate's name from passing through your lips. If you value being a member of this pack, you will wipe her from your thoughts as well.

Do you think you have the market cornered on grief, Sally? Do you think you're the only one who suffered when Millie was taken from us? You don't, and you're not. Me being blessed with a second chance with my fatal mate doesn't mean I didn't love your daughter.

It doesn't mean I didn't cherish what we had, or mourn her and our unborn pup. The difference is, I'm no longer wallowing in my grief. I've accepted the goddess's will. As such, I won't allow you to create an environment where my mate and our pups don't feel welcome in their pack."

Glenn may as well have not been separating them when Rosco's expression hardened and he took a step forward.

"Listen to me and hear me well, Sally Swift. If you wish to remain on these lands, you will keep a civil tongue in your head and stay away from me and my family."

Glenn's voice was firm but respectful when he asked, "what does that mean, Rosco? Are you saying we'll have to leave CVP lands?"

"No. If things don't change, Sally will have to leave. Not you. Not Shep or Silas. Unless you *want* to follow her to a new pack or into the human world."

It was a miracle from the goddess that Sally's gasp didn't suck all the oxygen from the room.

"What?! I was *born* into this pack. I was here long before you kicked your way into the world. And you think you have the right to demand *I* leave? Simply because I don't accept the female you're trying to replace my Millie with?"

Rosco was long past tired of this discussion, and his wolf agreed.

"I have every right. As Beta, it's my duty to protect the pack—whether it includes eliminating a physical threat or someone who interferes with pack unity.

But more than that, I have a responsibility to my mate and our pup. One I place first, above anything else. No harm will come to either of them. Not while I breathe. Having her not feel welcomed and accepted by her new pack would harm her. And I won't stand for it.

So, you make your decision now. Will you allow your hurt and pride to rule you? Do you really desire to start a new life without the support of this pack? The only place you've called home for more than sixty summers?"

With each sentence he spoke, Sally's expression vacillated between fury and desperation. When he was done, her gaze swung around the room wildly. It was obvious she was searching for allies.

She found none. Even with the size of the Carnahan family. The family of her birth. Sally didn't have anyone come to her defense. Not a single soul.

"Don't look at them. They won't help you. They know the rules the same as you. This will be the last time I speak on it. Get your shit together or leave."

Making eye contact with the silent Glenn, Rosco turned on his heel. Reclaiming his seat at Rahm's right hand, he set his overturned chair back on four legs before sitting. With the briefest of glances to the pack alpha, he nodded.

"I've said my piece."

Sally's sputtering was immediately quieted by her husband, who maneuvered her back into the seats they'd vacated. She looked far from happy, but she kept her mouth closed.

In his periphery, Rosco noticed Rahm scanning the room. It appeared he was making certain to capture the gaze of each shifter present.

"Just so we're clear. I stand with my beta. Anyone. No matter who they are. *Anyone*, who purposely seeks to disrupt pack unity won't be tolerated here. They *will* be stripped of CVP protection and escorted off our land."

With his hand balled into a loose fist, Rahm delivered two sharp raps to the tabletop.

"We're done here."

The silence was deafening as everyone filed from the room. Although both their mothers hung back to give Rosco hugs and assurances, they didn't say much. Well, not much beyond offering again to speak to Sally in a language she understood.

Declining their proposal to beat Sally to within an inch of her existence, Rosco followed them from the meeting hall. By the time they made it outside, the Swifts and Carnahans were nowhere to be found. Most of the crowd had disbursed. So, he and Rahm made the short walk back to their office.

"I know you have a soft spot for Millie's folks, but you should prepare yourself. She's not going to listen."

Flicking his gaze to Rahm before returning it to the empty road, Rosco nodded.

"I know. That show was more so for her family to know how serious I am about protecting mine, and for her to see even her mate wouldn't be able to save her from herself."

"Way to make a man feel like a man, Ros." Rahm shook his head. "And I thought you liked Glenn."

Rosco was certain it didn't make Glenn feel great to know, in this situation, he couldn't protect his own wife. But, it wasn't Rosco's problem to solve. Deanna came first. She and their pup were now his whole world.

"No matter how I feel about Glenn. No one comes before my mate. No one."

Chapter Thirteen

Although Deanna had become more than accustomed to doing things on her own, it was nice to have Breena want to take her around and introduce her to people. She had no obligations with Hannah running the Inn and the remainder of the furniture yet to be delivered. With nothing left to do to organize her new home, Deanna simply went with her new sister's suggestion to go outside and get to know the members of her new pack.

Considering her reception from Sally Swift, the mother of Rosco's first mate, Deanna was understandably concerned if she would be accepted by some of the pack members. After all, she'd gleaned that Sally's family had a long history in CVP. History tended to entail alliances.

It was one of the reasons she felt she couldn't stay in Blacktooth Summit once she broke her mate bond with Barry. His family had a connection to the Quinlin's with one of his ancestors being the pack beta before the alpha line started having their sons and brothers as betas, solidifying their position of future alphas being of the Quinlin line.

Despite how long ago it was, the number of generations that passed didn't diminish the importance the Thornes placed on the role one of their forebearers played in Blacktooth summit pack history. They'd even hinted at being part of the bloodline through one of the rare female Quinlin's. However, since the last female born in the line had been countless summers ago, no one could prove or disprove it without using a human DNA test.

"Lei-Lei, you know your mama doesn't like it when you dig around in her carrots. Come from over there."

Milagros Taiwo barely raised her voice, but the little silvery-gray wolf pup popped her little head up above the green shoots at the edge of the garden bed. There was a low barrier separating it from the rest of the expansive yard, but it wasn't a deterrent for the inquisitive pup. After a moment of hesitation, she lowered her nose as if in preparation to resume her digging around.

"Aht! If I get up and come over there, we're gonna have a problem, Miss Missy."

With a whining yip, the little wolf turned away from the garden. Before she made it to where her brother was rolling in the grass trying to capture his tail, she'd shifted into a fluff of brown bear cub. She immediately hopped onto the lion cub to aid him in apprehending the evasive appendage.

A giggle escaped Deanna's lips as she watched them. She'd always loved hanging around the nursery helping with the pups. She'd soured on the experience once the summers started adding up, and her womb remained empty of her own offspring. Barry had gotten nastier with each passing season without her going into heat.

So, attending the pups of others lost its luster. Deanna sought out different ways to spend her time and contribute to the pack. It hadn't mattered—to her mate nor her family.

Things were different now. The goddess had revealed to her the path which led her to her fatal mate. The womb once considered barren, now bloomed with new life. Watching the cubs tussle in the grass brought her a joy she'd forgotten existed.

"Anyway... So, we were talking about your travels and how you ended up in itty bitty Cummings, less than twenty miles from your wolf. It's fascinating."

Milagros regarded her with vibrant eyes filled with expectation.

Breena had wandered away after Marigold, Rahm's sister, stopped by. The two put their heads together giggling. Simply looking at them, it was easy to see they were thick as thieves. Near the same age, the major difference between them was Breena was already mated while Marigold was still finding her way.

Although she'd only gotten the story in snippets, Deanna's heart went out to Marigold. Her mother was the poster child for humans who shouldn't procreate—especially not with shifters when they couldn't or wouldn't learn enough to teach their child about both sides of their heritage.

At Milagro's prompting stare, Deanna resumed talking about the summers between when she left Blacktooth Summit before landing in Cummings. Of course, she glazed over her reasons for leaving. Carleeta's mother was still acclimating to life amongst shifters. Her husband was born a member of CVP, but had only spent part of his childhood there before moving away.

"Living among humans was an adjustment to the senses," Deanna began.

Nodding in understanding, Milagros gave her a sympathetic smile. "Oh, I'm sure. When Carleeta fully came into her shifter senses, she complained about smells and hearing sounds that I couldn't. It was good she had Rahm to help her adjust. You were out in the human world alone. It had to be hard."

Tamping down the swell of emotion, Deanna nodded. Her beast stirred trying to determine if there was danger, but Deanna was able to calm her before the feelings grew to the point of transmitting to her mate via their link. It had been less than ten minutes since she'd assured Rosco she was fine without being on protection duty.

"It was. At first. But once I learned some coping tools, I was proud of myself for being able to handle it on my own. I'm not now nor was I ever exiled from Blacktooth Summit. I could've gone home at any time. I didn't want to.

I enjoyed the freedom I had to explore and learn about myself and this vast continent. I even worked in a human bakery for a while. It was fun. If not for my shifter metabolism, I probably would've doubled my size. Which is saying something considering the abundance the goddess gave me to start with."

With a chuckle, Deanna glanced down at her thick thighs before smiling at Milagros.

"Oh, you must have learned some great baking tips."

Milagros leaned forward and their discussion ventured off the original path. They were considering the various uses for applesauce in cookies and cakes when Carleeta and Portia joined them. Each of them carried a tray.

"We thought you two would like something to drink and nibble on."

The duo set the trays on the two sturdy, almost waist high, tables, before Carleeta grabbed a couple of long t-shirts and held them up. Apparently, the cubs were used to the routine because they immediately shifted and toddled over to be dressed before their mother handed them the lidded cups designed for their small hands.

Accepting a frosted glass and a plate from Portia, Deanna perused the offerings. Making her selection from the variety of meats, cheeses, breads and crackers, she extended her appreciation.

"Thank you. I hadn't thought about eating, but the second I caught the scent, my stomach rumbled."

"It's not a problem. You and Mama were out here with these two titans of terror. Fixing you a snack was the least I could do."

"But you two are the one's heavy with cubs." Deanna felt a twinge of guilt as she watched Carleeta and Portia lower themselves into the lawn chairs.

"Don't worry about us. We're good." Carleeta flicked a lever on the side of her chair and a small platform slid forward from beneath it. Resting her feet on it, she grabbed her own drink.

"Speak for yourself." Portia released a light grunt as she adjusted herself in the chair on the other side of Milagros. "You're used to carrying Rahm's giant offspring. This is my first pregnancy, and it feels like there's more than one shifter standing on my bladder for most of the day."

Intrigued, Deanna lowered her glass and stared at Portia. "Are you having twins?"

Looking at the cubs, who were busy with both hands full of snack and drink, Deanna wondered if multiples were common in the pack in general, and in Rahm's family in particular.

"No, ma'am!" Portia quickly responded. "I checked for myself. Kellian has gotten better with the sonogram machine, but I wanted to be sure I didn't get tricked by synced heartbeats. So, I'm positive. This is just one extra-large passenger I'm carrying around."

Deanna's smile was automatic. Portia's description of her condition brought giggles bubbling up and out when combined with her facial expressions. One thing she missed moving around the way she had for the past five summers was having fellow shifter females to speak to regularly.

Although her departure from her pack showed her how fragile her relationships within it were, she still missed the fellowship. While she had many things in common with human females, connecting with them wasn't the same. They could only understand so much about her life. Besides, she didn't stay anywhere longer than eight months before she moved to Cummings.

"Isn't there some kind of rule about doctor's practicing on themselves?"

Carleeta's bright blue eyes sparkled, clearly showing her enjoyment of teasing her friend.

"I'm a vet." Portia wore a deadpan expression. Flipping her hand, she plucked a piece of yellow cheese from her plate and popped it into her mouth. "Besides, those are human rules. And, since it's been established that I'm a shifter, they don't apply to me."

"That's the story you're going with?" Laughter coated Carleeta's words.

"Those are the facts as I know them. And if you want me to waddle around your bedroom helping Mama Ley with delivery, you should stop while you're ahead. Because there are also rules about practicing on family—Niece."

"You're her aunt? I thought you were best friends. You look the same age."

Portia's statement caught her so off guard, Deanna blurted the question without thinking of whether it might be rude. Clamping her hand over her mouth, her eyes rounded.

"I'm sorry! I didn't mean it the way it sounded. I know there are mothers and daughters having off spring who are close in age. I let my mouth run off and leave my brain behind."

All three women burst into laughter with Portia waving off Deanna's embarrassment.

"You weren't rude, and I wasn't offended. It's a running joke between us. We are the same age. Roughly. I have a couple of years on her. And, we *are* best friends.

But, this is CVP. Here, there's no such thing as in-laws the way humans see it. Once you're mated, your family becomes his and vice versa. My mate, Brody, is Rahm's uncle. So, when we mated, I became his aunt." Tilting her head toward Carleeta she continued. "And hers."

"I don't care what you say, I'm not calling you Auntie." Carleeta's quip was accompanied by a flip of her wrist before she raised her glass to take a sip of the cool drink.

Deanna's question allowed the conversation to segue into a discussion about acclimating to the pack. Although her situation wasn't the same as theirs, with them living in the human world all of their lives, it was similar enough for them to have things in common.

She was pleased Carleeta seemed to have no ill-will toward her. Deanna had been told about Millie and Carleeta's relationship. How the two had grown close, and Rosco's first mate helped Carleeta connect better with her beast. It was refreshing to be accepted by someone who'd also loved Millie.

Maybe it was because she'd once been an outsider or it was simply Carleeta's nature to be welcoming, but Deanna appreciated it. Shortly after the twins climbed into their mother's and grandmother's laps, respectively, the conversation hit a lull. It was then that Deanna felt a surge of anger.

It wasn't her own, so it could only belong to Rosco. Her beast stood on alert in her mind. The feeling didn't ebb, causing her wolf to become agitated.

Something is wrong. Our mate is angry.

I feel it too.

Deanna considered reaching out to Rosco, but she knew the role of pack beta came with responsibilities which could put him in situations where his anger was sparked. If he was in the midst of a tense moment, she didn't want to distract him. Distractions could lead to injuries.

Are we going to do nothing? His anger is deep. Strong. He may need us.

What can we do? Reaching out to him could cause him to lose focus. He could be hurt.

So, we're doing nothing?

Her wolf's tone was filled with judgment.

Not nothing. We're waiting. If he stays angry or gets worse, I'll reach out to him. But not yet.

Despite the lip service she gave her wolf. Deanna sent what she hoped were feelings of calm through their link. She trusted he'd feel it, and it could bring him a modicum of relief.

Thankfully, she was able to maintain her composure, so the others didn't notice her distress. Less than an hour later, Breena returned without Marigold, who'd gone to the diner to help out.

Breena's eyes were bright as they bounced around the group, not looking at anyone for too long. Deanna and her new sister were still getting to know one another, but she sensed there was something Breena wanted to say, but didn't want to discuss it in front of the others.

Standing from the comfortable lawn chair, Deanna thanked Carleeta and her mother for their hospitality before offering to help with the clean-up. She was promptly waved off. At which point she said goodbye before she and Breena walked to the little bridge spanning the creek between the Alpha and Beta houses.

Once they were safely across and inside the house, Deanna tilted her head toward Breena. She'd barely gotten the question out before Breena spilled it all.

Holding up one hand, Deanna felt behind her, for the edge of the sofa to sit down.

"He did what? To who?"

"Rosco told Sally Swift that if she didn't stop running her mouth about the two of you—namely you—she would be kicked out of the pack."

Breena was apparently so excited about relaying the news, she didn't pick up on Deanna's stricken expression immediately. When she did, she sat next to Deanna.

"I didn't mean to upset you. He's probably gonna tell you about it, and explain why. But you won't hear what the other pack members thought from him. I was with Marigold at the diner when people started filing in talking about it."

Taking Deanna's left hand, Breena covered it with both of hers. "Don't feel bad for Sally. She was wrong for the way she treated you and my brother. Rosco was well within his right as your mate and our pack beta. The folks talking in the diner said as much.

I don't have very many memories of the time before Rahm became the pack alpha. I was really young. I heard things got bad under Champ. Really bad. So, when Rahm took over and started the council, one of the rules they passed was about pack unity.

Anyone who purposely set out to disrupt pack unity could be kicked out of the pack. There's a process. They have to be called before the council first. That's what happened with Sally today. She doesn't have to leave right this minute. If she stops her vendetta, she can stay. But if she doesn't..."

Breena let the rest of her statement hang in the air between them. Deanna was stunned. CVP operated unlike any pack she'd ever heard of. Sure, Blacktooth Summit had a council of elders, but the final decision on anything rested with the alpha. The only way to overrule him was to challenge him for the job.

Breena's excitement in the retelling bordered on gleeful which was contradictory to the kind she-wolf Deanna had considered her to be thus far. However, it appeared Sally had made it a point to spread her misery around. It was really unfortunate, since it seemed to go against the family togetherness which was apparent among many of the pack members Deanna had met so far.

While Breena was giving her a second hand blow-by-blow of the council meeting, Deanna had a revelation regarding the strong feelings of anger she'd felt from Rosco earlier. She now had context for the feeling. It made her and her beast more eager to see and talk to her mate. However, she quieted her beast, telling herself she needed to wait for Rosco to return home first.

"Hey, DK. Are you okay?" Concern put a crease in the otherwise smooth space between Breena's eyebrows.

Deanna thought she hid her anxiousness well. Breena's question made her realize her attempt at a neutral expression failed.

"I'm fine." Deanna knew the smile didn't reach her eyes, but it was the best she could muster.

Wrapping her fingers around the hands Deanna had clasped together in her lap, Breena's face softened. Her chocolate brown eyes projected her concern.

"I'm so oblivious! I'm sorry. Growing up with my brothers, I got so excited about having a sister again, I guess I got carried away."

Turning her hands over, Deanna delivered a quick squeeze to Breena's digits.

"No. Don't. You didn't do anything wrong. My thoughts drifted to something else. I promise. It's not you."

Wearing an earnest expression, Breena stared at her for a few silent beats. "Ok. If you say so."

"I do." Presenting a more believable smile, Deanna tapped the back of Breena's hand. "Now, tell me what else you and Marigold got up to."

Happy to oblige with the subject change, Breena launched into the other pack gossip she'd heard while helping Marigold in the diner. None of it was salacious, nor was it nearly as mean spirited as the things Sally had to say about Deanna and Rosco. However, it kept her entertained until it was time for Breena to go home to prepare for the arrival of her own mate.

By the time Deanna felt her mate getting closer and heard his steps on the porch, the evening meal was ready. Occupying the window seat offering the best view of the forest bordering one side of the Beta house, Deanna waited for Rosco to actually appear.

It was only after he came into her physical line of sight that she was able to release a little of the anxiety she'd held after learning the details of the council meeting. However, having her concerns assuaged didn't do anything for the twinge of...hurt?...anger? or was it frustration she felt about him excluding her from the council meeting? He'd neglected to tell her it wasn't a closed meeting and she could be present.

Rosco's long strides ate up the distance between them. While his face gave nothing away, his feelings rolled off him in waves. When he was within range, he leaned over her, capturing her lips in a barely chaste kiss.

"I apologize, Kitty Kat."

Chapter Fourteen

"Don't you Kitty Kat me, Rosco Greywolf."

A flame was banked behind Deanna's large brown eyes. A shiver of uncertainty skated across Rosco's skin warning him of his precarious position. He'd been certain of what he felt from her through their bond, but his mate's words indicated there was more than what he'd sensed.

Part of him was proud of her for not immediately acquiescing when he apologized for his unspoken slight. But, the other part was hoping simply expressing his regret would be enough. Her refusal of his pet name carried a little sting.

Sighing, he lifted her from the bench seat before sitting and draping her legs across his lap.

"Okay, Mate. Let's talk about why you want to revoke my privileges."

"I didn't say anything about revoking privileges. But, don't come in apologizing to me with sweet names when you intentionally set out to keep me in the dark."

"I didn't lie to you."

"Lies of omission are still lies, Rosco. You told me you were going to bring up Sally stealing the blanket and her behavior at the council meeting. You didn't say anything about giving her an ultimatum and possibly kicking her out of the pack. You definitely omitted the part where I'm allowed to attend the council meetings—even if I can't vote.

To make it worse, you closed yourself off from me. One moment I could feel you. Feel everything. The next, our connection was dull. Like there was a thick veil between us. I told myself it was because you were working and needed to shield me from those things. But, then I was hit with deep anger from you. I didn't put the puzzle together until Breena told me what she'd overheard in the diner."

Being physically close to her made it impossible for him to hide the jolt of irritation he experienced from learning his little sister had taken it upon herself to inform his mate of the happenings in the pack.

"Don't you go blaming Breena. I shouldn't have had to hear it from her. *You* should've told me yourself. Better yet, I should have been there. Beside you. To face the issue together. I thought that's what mates were supposed to do."

Turning her accusing stare away from him, Deanna's body was stiff, and her back was straight. She held herself away as if she didn't want to lean on him in the slightest. Inside him, his wolf was pacing. Neither of them liked being at odds with their mate.

"I didn't want you to worry about it. I also didn't want to subject you directly to hearing any of the bullshit Sally might've said. It was bad enough for her to say it to me. If you'd been present, I can't say what I would've done if I felt one sliver of sadness from you because of her.

As it was, I had moments where I could barely contain my beast. Had she said one word directly to you, I have no doubt I would've lost my shit."

Simply considering the possibility almost caused a resurgence of the fury he'd felt earlier. Deanna's brow bunched and her lips pinched together before she released them.

"I'd worry more, knowing you're finding ways to keep things from me than I will if I see and hear them for myself."

From the moment they'd met, Deanna had always looked at him without guile. Whatever her thoughts and feelings were, they were written in her expression and sensed through their bond. Even now, he could tell her anger was more hurt and disappointment than anything.

"Also, I have a question for you, Rosco Greywolf."

Rotating in his hold, she laid her hands on his shoulders as she straddled his lap with her knees pressing into the padding on either side of his hips. "While you were busy trying to protect me from malicious barbs and potential emotional harm, who was protecting *you*? Who was guarding against those things for you?"

Rosco had no answer to her question, and she knew it. Because, while he had something of a support system present, none of them saw the need his mate had latched onto with her query. He wasn't fighting a physical battle, but an emotional one. And he'd excluded his mate from shoring him up during that time.

Dropping his forehead to hers, he didn't disguise the sentiment pulsing through their bond. His eyelids slid closed as he spoke to her over their link.

"There was no one there, because it should've been you. I know that. I robbed you of your right, Mate. I'm sorry isn't enough to make up for it, but an apology with a promise is all I have."

Deanna's soft hand cradled the side of his face and her fingertips skimmed his low, scruffy beard. He sensed her acceptance before she actually spoke.

"I am your mate, Rosco. And, as big and bad as you are, even **you** *need someone to look out for you."*

Deep coffee colored-eyes bore into his. *"As much as I am yours, you are* **mine**. *We are in this together. Remember?"*

Deanna reminding him they belonged to one another had an effect he was certain she didn't intend. But, there was something about hearing her declare him as hers... It went straight to his shaft, causing it to thicken in his pants.

Her scent hit him a split second before she rotated her hips, grinding her heated core against his stiffening length. The barrier of their clothing did nothing to obstruct, while simultaneously making it impossible to enjoy the full effect of their position.

Mine! His beast rumbled inside him.

Yes, beast. Ours.

Rosco was certain his feral instincts were plainly written on his face. Lust descended, dropping his eyelids as he zeroed in on the pulse beating at the base of Deanna's neck. It telegraphed her desire as clearly as the fragrance wafting from her slickening folds. He didn't need to see it to know her essence was flowing in preparation to be tasted then taken.

How could he deny his mate what her body obviously wanted? Needed. He couldn't. In a swift motion, which drew a startled squeaking, gasp from his mate, Rosco deposited her on the bench once more. Only with far less material between her ass and the seat cushion.

Dropping to his knees on the floor between her spread legs, he dragged one fingertip down the seam of her puffy folds. Evidence of her desire shined when he split the crease, exposing her bright pink center. Licking his lips, he spared one final glance at her beautiful face before he placed his nose to her pearl then dipped his tongue into her channel.

"Mine!"

Rosco growled his claim through their mate link. Having the ability to speak to her while his mouth was busy dispensing pleasure added a layer to their coupling he had no idea was missing.

"Mmm... Yes, Big Bad. Yours..."

Deanna's immediate agreement, combined with the way she yielded to him served to feed Rosco's possessive, determined drive to please her. This wasn't about heat or mate bonding. It was about the two of them —their bodies needed to connect to one another.

Her fingers tugged at the short strands of his hair as he dined on her ambrosia, giving her no relief from his pleasurable assault. The flavor of her juices was almost as addictive as having her velvet core wrapped about his length. The length which was throbbing within the confines of his pants, begging to be released.

When the light tugs became more urgent, Rosco didn't deny her silent request. He practically ripped through his pants to free his stiffness before sitting back on his haunches and pulling Deanna from the bench directly onto his hard shaft.

He supplied her replacement breaths when her mouth dropped with a gasping inhale from being filled so quickly. His mate's tight sheath gripped his cock to the point he wasn't sure he'd be able to stop himself from bathing her insides with his seed after a few thrusts. The sensations where nearly overwhelming.

Feeling their emotional connection while being physically

connected to Deanna was fucking with his head, but Rosco didn't want to be free from it. In fact, he wanted to be closer. He wanted to soak in it and have it draped across him like armor.

As much as he wanted their coupling to last, he knew his time was limited. Leaning her backwards, he delivered a suckling nibble to her nipple, causing a gush of slickness from her core, drowning his shaft in her sweet nectar.

"Rosco!"

Deanna's cry simultaneously pierced the air and vibrated over their link. Transferring his hold to her hips, Rosco let go and began thrusting wildly. He soon joined her with his own climax, pumping his seed deep into her already fertilized womb.

Breathing heavily, he gathered her close, cradling her to his chest. With a kiss to the top of her head, he rested his chin there for a few moments, simply enjoying the sound of their synchronized heartbeats and the feeling of having his mate in his arms.

He knew he was only temporarily sated and would want her again later. But for now, he was content to hold her in his arms while his cock softened but remained cocooned in her warmth.

"Thank you, Mate." Rosco murmured into the crown of Deanna's thick hair.

Her reply was delayed and slightly groggy. "Mmm. Thank me for what?"

"For being with me. For seeing the things I don't admit aloud. And... for being you."

Shifting, she stared into his eyes with her far-too-penetrating gaze. "You're welcome, but you don't have to thank me for being myself. I don't know how to be anyone else."

After Millie's death, Rosco sincerely never thought he'd feel the same depth of happiness again. Yet, here he was a wolf mated for more than five moons to his fatal mate. A she-wolf who seemed to have a never-ending pool of patience and kindness.

Those characteristics didn't mean she was a pushover, because

Deanna gave as good as she got. Although they didn't have many serious disagreements to speak of. Rosco found himself settling into mated life quite well. For the most part, things were going great.

He was loving the opportunity to watch Deanna's belly harden and expand as their future grew inside her womb. He was never more grateful Brody's mate, Portia, had joined Kellian in serving as pack doctor. After observing her examination of Deanna, Rosco was certain he would've broken each of Kellian's fingers, individually, before performing the same with the male's arms.

Having Portia perform the checks and tests was the best possible outcome for all involved. For Rosco, the highlight of that and future visits was seeing the images on the screen. It was a blessing from the goddess he was sitting the first time.

Three Months ago

"BB, you can't keep growling at the doctor any time he looks in my direction. He's just doing his job."

Deanna spoke over their link to keep their conversation private. Rosco didn't care if Kellian heard him. He wanted the other shifter to know how he felt about his mate being touched by another male. However, to appease his mate, he responded using the link.

"Doc Portia is here for you. What's his purpose for being in the room?"

Soft fingers covered his where they lay clenched on the examination table beside her.

"Remember, Doc Portia is still in training. She's an animal doctor. We're shifters, but we're not animals. He has to be here to help her."

"How is he helping her? He doesn't even know how to use that contraption she's fiddling with. To me, it looks like she's training him. Can't they do that some other time? On some other patient?"

"Rosco... Behave."

Lucky for him, he didn't have time to respond because Doc Portia turned toward them and began explaining what she was going to do next. Then, they were both completely consumed by the image on the monitor.

As she moved the arrow shaped pointer around on the screen, Rosco had to rub his eyes to clear them to be certain of what he was seeing. When the doctor flipped a switch and the sound of rapid thumps filled the room, he tugged at his ears to clear them because he couldn't be hearing what she said they should hear.

Two...There were two... According to Doc Portia, there were two sepa-rate heartbeats. Twins. His vision fogged over and Rosco's own heartbeat was so loud it blocked him from hearing anything else.

"Rosco? Rosco?" Deanna's urgent calling of his name jerked him back into the moment. Clearing his vision, he transferred his gaze to his mate's concerned face.

"Yes?"

"Are you okay? It looked like you'd taken a journey without leaving the room."

Lifting her hand, he kissed the back of it. "There is nowhere I ever intend to go that I can't take you with me. I was just surprised. Before today, when I heard the pup's heartbeat, it sounded like only one."

Briefly, he wondered if something really was wrong with his hearing. How hadn't he heard the second heartbeat? Not one to dwell on unknowns when he could have his question answered, Rosco asked the doctor.

"How is it that I can hear the two different heartbeats now, and I couldn't before."

"Sometimes, the heartbeats are so closely synced it sounds like one. Espe-cially when they're this young and their pulse is so rapid. If it weren't for the machine, and us being able to see the two little beans, we might not have been able to detect them both."

Her explanation made him feel better. He hadn't made it this far in the process with Millie and their pup. Also, Doc Portia hadn't brought her human technology with her until later. So, this was a first for him and Deanna.

Once she was certain he was okay, Deanna returned to staring at the monitor as Doc Portia moved the pointer around and pressed buttons. He was torn between watching the awe on his mate's face and staring at the screen holding her in its thrall.

Present

Rosco strode down the path of stones he'd laid, which led from the back door of the Beta house to the wooden bridge spanning the creek separating their home from the Alpha house. The sun was high in the sky, but it wasn't doing much to ward off the cold temperature. Since his body ran hot, he wasn't bothered. A light jacket was all which was required.

His mate, on the other hand, was a different story. Normally very responsible, she had left without her coat earlier that morning. His sister had picked her up after he'd already gone. Deanna still didn't drive much around pack lands.

The only time she attempted it was when she had to go into Cummings. Even then, she ended up being driven by him or a member of the security force. Rosco didn't care how irrational anyone said he was, she wasn't allowed to travel outside the distance of their link without him, or at least someone, to protect her, along with carrying one of the pocket telephones Carleeta insisted they get.

Especially not when he was suspicious of every stranger who came through Cummings and stopped for more than a day. He hadn't forgotten the day he'd moved Deanna from the Inn to CVP lands. She believed she was mistaken when she'd mentioned seeing someone familiar.

It's possible she didn't know the wolf who was hanging around inside the hardware store. However, Rosco wouldn't take any chances. Robeson had reported back on the stranger. He informed Rosco the wolf shifter hadn't stayed more than a few hours before getting into a pickup and driving in a direction away from pack lands.

The security team was on a rotating schedule to keep an eye on things in Cummings, and there hadn't been any other sightings. But, there had been a few inquiries made at the Inn as to Deanna's where-abouts. They'd all been phone calls. According to Hannah, it wasn't the same person each time and she'd simply passed the message on to Deanna.

Thankfully, she didn't give any information beyond saying Deanna wasn't available at the moment and offering to take a message. Whoever was hoping to speak to his mate, never left one, which made Rosco even more suspicious.

His mate swore she had no idea who it could be as she'd made very few friends who didn't live in Cummings. She had no contact with anyone from Blacktooth Summit, and she'd already reconnected with the humans befriended during her tour of the continent. So, they knew of her relocation.

Rosco pushed open the back door to the Alpha house and stepped inside. Even being at the rear of the house, the sounds of an active household reached his ears. As he walked up the long hallway, Rahm strode out from one of the rooms with an infant strapped to his chest. In a rare occurrence, a non-shifted, fully clothed Echo was latched to his father's leg.

Rahm moved as if he didn't have nearly fifty pounds attached to his calf. Stopping a few feet away from Rosco, he gave him a questioning look. Instead of a verbal answer, Rosco held up the coat he held fisted in one hand. With a nod, Rahm jerked his head toward the front of the house, although Rosco already had a decent idea of where Deanna was.

Before he walked across the bridge, Rosco could've reached out via their link to find out Deanna's exact location inside the Alpha House. But, he didn't. It was a large house, but not so large, he couldn't sniff out his mate.

When he entered the room, the conversation came to a halt.

"Don't let me interrupt. I'm just here to bring my mate something she left behind."

Despite his comment, they remained silent. Although he didn't check to be certain, he felt all five pairs of eyes on him as he crossed the room to where Deanna was sitting on a sofa next to Breena.

Dropping a kiss on his mate's forehead, Rosco placed the coat on the arm of the couch before placing one hand on her rounded belly.

"I told you I was fine without this big thing."

"And I told you it was too cold for you to be galivanting all over the place without it."

With a quick kiss to her pouting lips, he stood to his full height, nodded to the others, and strode from the room. As he left, he sent a parting directive via their mate link.

"Let me know when you're ready to go home."

Chapter Fifteen

Deanna couldn't believe Rosco. She wasn't a youngling who needed their parent to show up at their school to bring them the lunch they forgot at home. Granted, she *was* cold on the short walk from Breena's car at each stop. But, it was only for a quick second.

As a wolf shifter, one would think her blood ran hot enough for her to walk around like some others—without a big outer coat. Deanna could only do that in her wolf form. In her humanoid form, she required a light jacket if the wind blew too strongly. So, she should've been grateful her mate had noticed she'd forgotten her coat and brought it to her.

"You might as well quit pouting. It won't stop him from treating you like you're made of glass."

Carleeta's expression was one of understanding, even if she was calling Deanna out for pouting like the youngling she'd just told herself she wasn't.

"I'm not pouting."

"Sure...whatever you say, DK."

Deanna preferred the other look Carleeta had given over the smirk she wore following Deanna's denial of the pout. It didn't matter that her friend was correct. She didn't have to say it aloud.

"Anyway, let's get back to the topic at hand." Portia shifted the infant she'd just finished breastfeeding.

The little princess's lips were still pursed as if she was trying to decide if she was upset about her meal being over. Before she could make up her mind, or release more than a disgruntled whimper, Portia's mate strode into the room.

For someone so large, he was exceedingly gentle when lifting the youngling. Holding her to his chest with one massive hand, he leaned over, giving Portia a kiss before leaving. Deanna observed Portia watching her mate. Carleeta leaned over and snapped her fingers in front of her friend's face.

"Focus! The big bear walked in, and you forgot what you were going to say."

Waving Carleeta's hand away from her face, a slight flush crept into Portia's cheeks. If Deanna had to guess, Portia's mate had said something over their mate link to garner the reaction. Of course, unless the fox shifter told the rest of them, they'd never know what it was.

When Portia regained her composure and started once again talking about the plans for the upcoming holidays, Deanna's mind drifted a bit. While commemorating Winter Solstice was common, celebrations of human holidays weren't much of a priority in her former pack. However, since relocating to the CVP, she realized they were a very eclectic bunch.

There were humans living among them—and not just those who'd mated shifters. So, they practiced some customs Deanna had only seen consistently observed by humans. It was unexpected.

Another phenomena, which took her by surprise, was the number of fatal matings in the pack. Honestly, Deanna had never considered she'd meet her fatal mate. She found it amazingly fascinating. She also now understood why some shifters refused to settle for any other kind of mating.

The discussion between Portia and the others surrounding the planning of festivities faded into the background as Deanna's mind drifted to how drastically her life had changed since she and Rosco mated. Their relationship made her previous one with Barry seem even more hollow and unfulfilling. Now, she couldn't imagine willingly accepting such a union.

"What do you think, DK?"

Carleeta's question snatched Deanna back into the discussion. The last thing she'd vaguely heard was something about activities for the younglings. Hoping they were still talking about them, Deanna pasted a smile on her face and latched onto the topic.

"I'm happy to help with the younglings. We can get them started on some things in advance if it will help."

She breathed a sigh of relief when Carleeta simply thanked her before they moved on in the conversation. Despite not personally observing Christmas, Deanna was certain she knew enough or could find out enough to be able to guide the younglings in some activities.

Working at the pack school turned out to be exactly what she needed to help her integrate into the pack more. Having a formal degree in education, by human standards, wasn't a requirement. Although Deanna was educated in shifter and human studies. It was what she did with part of the funds Quinlan gave her when she struck out from the pack.

Leaving Blacktooth Summit was her choice; she wasn't kicked out or exiled. So, she was gifted with what was deemed necessary for her to make a new start in the place of her choice.

"Kitty Kat, are you ready to go home yet?"

Even though she gave an internal eye roll at his impatience, Deanna didn't ignore her mate.

"Not yet. We're still discussing the Winter Solstice and Christmas activities."

"You aren't volunteering for anything too strenuous are you?"

"Rosco...I'm a wolf. Not a porcelain doll. And no. I didn't volunteer for anything strenuous—unless you consider using glue to add sparkles to paper wreaths strenuous."

There was a moment of silence over their link where Deanna thought he'd gone back to whatever he was doing, and allowing her to resume her planning with the others. However, it appeared her mate wasn't done.

"Do you need me to relax you later?"

"What? Why would you ask me if I need relaxing? I'm not tense."

Deanna had no idea why Rosco would suggest such a thing, because she knew exactly what he meant by 'relax'. It didn't involve actual rest.

"Well..."

"Well what, Rosco?"

"You've been a little...testy lately."

"Me? Testy? I have not."

"Yeah... You kinda have. But, I don't want to argue. I was simply offering to help."

*"If I have any more of your **help**, I'll need to place my she-wolf bits into a rejuvenation chamber."*

Even as she denied his *assistance*, Deanna squirmed in her seat hoping she could keep calm enough not to embarrass herself by releasing the scent of her desire.

"A what?"

"It's a thing Portia and Carleeta told me about. It makes things like new."

"Kitty Kat... I don't think it's a real thing. Besides, I can kiss it and make it better."

That did it. The fragrance of her arousal hit her nose, and judging by the way Breena cut off mid-sentence, Deanna wasn't the only one to smell it.

"Rosco Greywolf!"

"Don't fuss, Mate. Put your coat on. I'm on my way to get you."

Due to their keen senses of sight, hearing and smell, shifters had very few secrets. Shame surrounding natural occurrences wasn't a thing. Yet, Deanna's entire face felt like it should be crimson red from the flames blazing beneath her skin. Her mortification was increased tenfold when Marigold lifted Deanna's discarded coat and held it up for her.

Her tongue was glued to the roof of her mouth. So, all Deanna could do was stand up and allow herself to be assisted into the garment. She had one sleeve on when Rosco's long strides brought him into the room again. Nodding to the others, he took over the task of getting her into the coat.

Mumbling an awkward goodbye and something she hoped sounded like a promise to check in with them, she rushed out of the house with her mate. While she was embarrassed, her wolf was practically dancing inside. She was completely enamored with their mate and thoroughly enjoyed any opportunity to couple.

It was why Deanna had experienced another first, with Rosco mounting her while they were both in their shifted forms. The lusty beast was anxious for the opportunity to do it again. Deanna's wolf had never been sexual before. Before Rosco, she'd thought her beast would only take an interest in the act if it involved a heat cycle. And since she hadn't gone into heat until she reached forty-five summers, Deanna didn't anticipate the wolf ever encouraging the activity.

A cold blast of wind hit Deanna's face making her close her eyes against it. It was enough to cool her ardor and make her snuggle deeper into the coat she'd claimed she didn't need. Without a word, her mate scooped her into his arms. The journey across the winter-hardened lawn and over the bridge was swift with his long legs eating up the distance.

They stepped inside to the ringing of the phone. Placing her on her feet, Rosco closed the door behind them before going to answer the call. His voice held its normal gruffness when he placed the receiver to his ear, stating his name as a form of greeting.

"Rosco."

Of course, with her enhanced hearing, Deanna was able to hear the other person clearly.

"Rosco, it's Glenn."

Rosco's eyes met Deanna's, and she instinctively moved closer to him. Their contact with Millie's parents had been minimal following the council meeting all those moons ago. While the Swifts and Carnahans as a whole seemed to give them a wide berth, Glenn was cordial and friendly when he encountered them.

"Hey, Glenn. Is something wrong? Something you need?"

Rosco had transitioned fully into pack beta mode. It wasn't unusual for a CVP member to call him or for Rahm to call and ask him to handle something—whether it be security related or some other issue.

"Well... You might not see it as something wrong. But I thought you should know. Sally has decided to leave."

Deanna felt simultaneously relieved and saddened to hear the news. Rosco's arms tightened around her, and she rested her head on his chest. The steady thud of his heart beneath her ear helped to sooth her as much as the sensations she received from him via their bond.

"I'm not sure what you want me to say, Glenn. It's been many moons since the council meeting. While I meant what I said, I was also sincere when I offered for her to remain, as long as she was civil. As far as I know, she's kept up her end. So, I had no plans of making a new case with Rahm and the council."

Glenn's voice sounded sad, but Deanna keyed in on the exact words he'd spoken. Tilting her head back, she connected her gaze to Rosco's.

"Glenn said Sally was leaving. What about him? And Silas? Are they leaving as well?"

"Those are good questions." Rosco's response over their link was followed by him relaying her questions to Glenn. Deanna's heart hurt for Glenn a little as she listened to his response.

"Son...you more than anyone know how hard it's been since we lost Millie."

Deanna slid her arms around Rosco, hugging him. While she knew he cared for her deeply, she also felt the hint of sadness invading his feelings at the mention of his first mate. Unaware of Rosco's moment of discomfort, Glenn continued.

"Sally seemed to be coping, a little melancholy at times, but coping. At least she was until you mated again. It seemed like something snapped inside her.

I don't recognize her, and she appears to be unable to see reason. She doesn't remotely resemble who I married and have spent most of my adult life with. I don't see how me and the boys uprooting our lives here will fix it. I've made a family here beyond her. Silas doesn't want to move to live so closely to humans either.

His shifter senses developed slowly. But now that they have, he has difficulty even going into Cummings with the sounds and smells most humans can't detect. I won't make him go. Shep has made it pretty clear he won't break from the pack. We all love her. However, this is one time, she'll have to find her way through it on her own. We can't fix it for her. So, for the time being, she'll be in Cummings. Maybe she'll come to her senses. I can't say right now."

Acknowledging Glenn's confession, Rosco nodded. "I wish it hadn't come to this, but thank you for letting me know."

"It was the least I could do. And, Rosco." Glenn paused. *"I hope you know I wish nothing but the best for you and Deanna. She seems to be a genuinely kind person. I'm glad you have another chance at happiness."*

Although Glenn hadn't made the exact statement, Deanna read between the lines that he still considered Rosco his son. And, as much as it pained him, he wasn't willing to follow his wife down a harmful path. She leaned against Rosco with her head on his chest listening to his heartbeat combined with the low rumble of his voice as he exchanged a few more words with Glenn before ending the call.

Needless to say, the interruption doused the flame of arousal which had her mate nearly sprinting to their home with her in his arms. However, Deanna wasn't disappointed. She and Rosco didn't have any issues in the area of wanting one another physically. What her mate needed from her at the moment, she offered freely.

While he wasn't as hard on himself as he had been in the beginning, there were still instances where he dropped into silence and she felt his guilt. It was usually when they had an experience he'd either not had with Millie or he seemed to enjoy more with Deanna. All she could do during those times was assure him that she didn't view his first mate as competition.

Her situation with Barry was decidedly different. So, there was never any guilt when she enjoyed an aspect of mating she hadn't previously. However, she was also learning not to compare the two. Barry hadn't been taken from her, and she felt no lingering love for him. But, she couldn't fault Rosco for the rare lapses.

From everything she'd learned, they'd had a loving relationship and he'd told her himself about her tragic demise. Any being would have difficulty moving past it. Especially a shifter who'd considered himself mated for life, only to have it ripped away from him.

As much empathy as she had for Rosco, Deanna wasn't saddened to hear Sally Swift would no longer be walking around pack lands shooting semi-glaring glances from afar. Nor would Deanna be standing in the aisle at the market and have Sally make a show of leaving.

Of course, she never spoke directly to Deanna. There was at least one part of Rosco's warning she took seriously. The instances weren't plentiful, but they happened often enough for Deanna to dread seeing her. It got worse as Deanna's belly began to swell with the pups.

Snuggling deeper into Rosco's embrace, Deanna murmured, "I'm sorry for Glenn, but I can't say I'm sorry to not encounter Sally as often anymore. Since I only go to Cummings once every couple of weeks to check in with Hannah at the Inn, our interactions will be cut down to almost zero."

Deanna tilted her face upward when Rosco pulled back slightly. She met his concerned expression and immediately knew she'd stepped into a pile of scat.

"Is there something you forgot to tell me, Mate?"

"No. I didn't forget. I just didn't think it bore mentioning that I wasn't very fond of running into Sally around Pack Town Center. She never said anything to me or about me within earshot. Considering I was aware of her feelings surrounding our mating, it was bound to be uncomfortable."

"I still would've preferred you'd told me about it."

"Why, BB? Were you going to kick her out of the pack because she didn't want to be in the same places as me? That wouldn't be right." When he bristled, she quickly slid her hands up to cradle his face. "And guess what? We don't have to have this conversation again, because she's not going to be around."

Issuing a low rumble of a grouse, Rosco let the matter drop. They both knew there was no point in arguing about the past when the situation was unlikely to occur in the future.

"Just know, you aren't to go into Cummings without me. Not even if you're going with Breena or Mom. It's me or you stay here."

Now it was Deanna's turn to bristle. "I beg your pardon, Rosco Greywolf? What you just said sounded an awful lot like an edict or mandate. I'm not a subject in your royal court. I'm your mate."

Whether she was right or wrong for not telling him about the occurrences, didn't give him the grounds to dictate to her. At least not in her opinion. Rosco's gaze narrowed as he stared at her. He didn't speak aloud, nor did he use their mate link. He simply stared at her at first.

The use of words wasn't necessary, because everything he felt was being transmitted via their bond. Yes, there was his frustration with her push back, but there was also his concern—which she knew was genuinely for her well-being. There was also the undercurrent of his possessiveness and determination.

"Mate... I am well aware of who you are. You are mine. As such, *I* protect you. *I* keep you and our pups safe. You don't have to like the way I said it, but know we cannot compromise on this. I cannot have you there without me—especially not now."

Without thought, Deanna's thumbs rubbed in circles along the tops of his shoulders where her hands now rested. She didn't consider Sally a physical threat. It wasn't likely Rosco did either. However, the wave of emotions she felt from him clamped her mouth closed.

He was naturally protective, but fear of losing her was laced through his being. If her conceding, yielding to one of the few demands he made would ease his fears, she'd do it.

Chapter Sixteen

Rosco and Rahm were walking out of the woods after their check of the northern border discussing changes in the patrols. It had been a few weeks since Glenn informed him of Sally moving to Cummings. Rosco wondered where she would live there as the only temporary housing he was aware of was the Inn Deanna owned. And he was positive Sally would never set foot in the place, knowing who the owner was—despite his mate's rare appearances there.

Glenn told him she'd secured a small cottage on the edge of town opposite pack lands. Her being able to find property made Rosco think she'd been planning her move for a while. Cummings was small, but their population remained pretty consistent.

That he knew of Vanessa, Marigold's birth mother, was the last to leave. However, there was a stretch of more than a year where he hadn't gone near the place. So, things could've occurred without his knowledge.

As he and Rahm cleared the edge of the tree line, drawing closer to the Alpha house, a transport truck was reversing next to the large bay doors of one of the outbuildings. It was the one Carleeta used for finished pieces and shipments of wood for her carpentry business.

They'd just come abreast of the vehicle when it rolled to a stop and the engine shut off. The driver's side door opened, and Trip hopped down from the cab.

"For a change, you two have great timing. I had to send the guys on another run." Looking between them, his gaze was directed mostly toward Rahm.

"You can help me unload this bocote your mate had me go all the way to Colombia to hand pick for her."

Trip's voice was rough with an edge of fatigue. Rosco almost felt sorry for him. Until he opened his mouth and was more Trip than usual.

"She owes me one. No. Two of those miracles after what I had to do to get this load." He tossed his demand over his shoulder as he walked toward the back of the trailer.

"My Beloved isn't a carnival show. She doesn't perform for anyone."

Rahm's hackles weren't completely up, as it was common for him and Trip to banter in a way which was borderline aggressive most days.

With his hand on the handle latching the door closed, Trip glared at Rahm.

"I'm not asking for an audience to watch her do it. Besides, this is a chip I'll cash in at a later date."

Trip threw the door open, momentarily disappearing behind it. Rosco and Rahm exchanged a look, but neither spoke. Since Trip owned an intercontinental transport business, he occasionally spent time away from the pack checking on those interests.

Although he'd respond to any request from Rahm and Rosco, he didn't make many personal trips to secure items. However, it wasn't unheard of. He'd been in more than a few hairy situations while on pack and personal business.

Rosco didn't have to think back very far to remember the jaunt they'd made together with a couple of the other guys to help Brody and had ended up on a rescue mission in a swamp filled with critters even shifters stay away from.

Whatever he'd experienced in Columbia must have been pretty bad if he's trying to extract payment beyond the normal costs incurred. Delivering a sharp headshake to Rosco, Rahm strode to the open trailer door.

They looked inside just as Trip tossed the last tarp off. Rosco had questions about why the wood was covered while inside a covered vehicle, but kept them to himself. The jaguar shifter wasn't his normal irreverent, sarcastic self. So, more than he wanted to push Trip's buttons, Rosco was curious about what happened on the cargo run.

The wood in question was strikingly gorgeous in its raw form. Whatever plans Carleeta had for it, the piece would be eye catching. Even if it was a plain chair—it would be the feature of any furniture grouping.

Waiting on the ground, he and Rahm hefted the lumber onto their shoulders when Trip passed it out to them. For the most part, they worked silently. However, as they were taking the last loads into the building, Trip got Rosco's attention.

"Hey, it's not my business, but I saw it. So, I'm gonna ask."

Arranging his load on the nearest stack, Rosco lifted a questioning eyebrow. Accepting the expression as permission, Trip kept talking.

"I'd heard about Sally Swift moving to Cummings, but I didn't know she'd set Glenn aside—broken their mate bond."

With a hand still on the pile, Rosco halted any movement. "To my knowledge they didn't break the bond."

Rosco knew Glenn was hoping she'd come to her senses and just needed some time. Whether it was likely to happen wasn't up to Rosco to say. So, he hadn't mentioned it further.

"They didn't?" Dusting his shirt and pants, Trip propped his foot on a different stack of less valuable wood and leaned on his knee. "Well, that makes me wonder then."

Rolling his eyes to the ceiling, Rosco asked the goddess for patience. Apparently unloading the truck had Trip feeling more like himself. Thankfully, Rahm was as much in the mood for Trip's shenanigans as Rosco was—which was not at all.

"You can get to the fucking point any second now."

Shooting Rahm a disgruntled glare, Trip looked back to Rosco. "I stopped in Cummings on my way home. I wasn't there long, but it was long enough to see Sally in the diner huddled close to another shifter. From the smell of him, he's not from around here, but the scent was vaguely familiar.

It took me until I hit the curve in front of Doc Portia's to place it. It was faint, but he smelled like those wolves from Blacktooth Summit. It didn't click until I saw Brody out in front of the house."

That got Rosco's full attention. "Are you certain it was Blacktooth Summit?"

"Positive."

Rosco glanced over to Rahm. He'd been beta to Rahm's alpha for so long, sometimes they didn't need to speak.

"I'll call him and get him over here." Taking long strides, Rahm left the two of them inside the storage building.

Confusion dipped Trip's brows. "What did I miss?"

"Deanna was a part of Blacktooth Summit. She grew up there."

"Okay..."

Trip wasn't following Rosco, and Rosco couldn't explain why he was so suspicious of an unknown male shifter being seen with Sally. And... said shifter faintly carrying the scent of Blacktooth Summit. It could be nothing. His intuition was telling him otherwise.

Heaving a breath, Rosco shared something he'd kept between him and Deanna. Neither of them had mentioned to anyone outside his immediate family, Rahm and Carleeta that she'd been mated previously.

"She was mated before. She severed the mate bond. It was long before she came here."

"Do you think someone from the pack has come to try to make her go back?"

Trip's question triggered a growl from Rosco's beast.

"They will have to kill me to take my mate." His beast's internal growling dripped on Rosco's every word.

Holding his hands up with his palms facing outward, Trip made a slight pushing motion.

"Whoa... I didn't mean to get you riled up. I was just trying to understand why someone from that pack would be so close to the CVP. He didn't look familiar. So, I'm sure we didn't meet him when we were there."

Dismissing Trip, Rosco reached out to Deanna using their mate link. He knew she was on pack lands, but she didn't feel as close as if she were at their home.

"Mate? Where are you? Are you okay?"

Deanna's response was immediate. *"I'm at the school. And I'm fine… but you feel… Worried? Angry? What's going on?"*

He'd hoped to keep her from feeling the full force of what he was experiencing, but Rosco guessed it was inevitable. He hadn't anticipated needing to put a block between them.

"It's nothing for you to worry about. I just wanted to know where you were. I'm at the Alpha house and didn't sense you at home."

"Oh, well I'm here helping the children with their craft projects for the Winter Solstice festival. Breena came to get me earlier. That's why I'm not home. I should only be here for another hour."

He purposely allowed her to think his concern was due to her being away from the Beta house. Wrapping up their silent communication with a promise to see her later, Rosco motioned to Trip as he followed the path Rahm had taken to the outside.

Less than twenty minutes later, they were seated in Rahm's home office as Brody asked Trip questions about what he'd seen. It made Rosco feel justified in his suspicions. So, he informed them of the previous instance of a stranger being in Cummings.

"The day I moved Deanna from the Inn into the Beta house, she said she thought she saw someone familiar. She brushed it off, but I had Robeson go back and look around. He didn't get a name, only said there was an unknown wolf shifter hanging around town, but the wolf didn't stay long."

"Do you think it's the same wolf?"

Rosco didn't believe it was possible for shifters, other than fatal mates, to read one another's mind, but Brody gave the impression he was sifting through Rosco's thoughts when he stared at him after asking the question.

"It's possible. It makes sense if she saw someone she knew, and there's an unknown shifter in Cummings carrying the scent of the Blacktooth Summit Pack."

Nodding, Brody reached into one of the many pockets on the utility pants he wore and pulled out a small black book. Flipping it open, he gestured to Rahm to slide the phone closer.

Like his nephew, Brody wasn't big on unnecessary talking. So, instead of speculating further, he picked up the phone receiver and punched a few keys. Rosco didn't have to wonder what he was doing because after just two rings, Jeffrey Quinlin's voice barked a hello.

"Quinlin. Parata here."

"What's wrong?"

There wasn't the normal banter between the two at Quinlin assuming there was a problem because Brody called him. Which was good, since it allowed Brody to get straight to the point.

"Is there a reason one of your pack members would be in the area? As in less than thirty miles away in the little town of Cummings?"

"Nope. No. I haven't sent anyone out in that direction. If I had, I would've made contact in advance. I have *some* sense of diplomacy."

"Well, you're not keeping good enough tabs on your pack members because there's a wolf hanging around Cummings who carries the Blacktooth scent."

A thudding sound came over the line as if Quinlin's feet had slammed onto the wooden floor Rosco remembered from being in his office. His already deep voice sounded as if he was chewing gravel when he next spoke.

"I don't tell you how to do whatever the fuck it is you do since you stopped hiding in your bear. You don't tell me how to be an alpha to my pack."

The two took a few shots at each other before Rahm intervened.

"Anytime you two want to stop measuring dicks we can talk about what *could* be going on. The reason Trip scented a Blacktooth Summit wolf in a town under CVP protection."

Rahm's interruption was apparently what they needed to get back on topic. There weren't many scenarios the group of them could come up with since, Quinlin was adamant all his folks were accounted for.

"Were you aware that Deanna Madkins relocated to Cummings almost two summers ago?"

Rosco was relieved when Brody's question didn't set Quinlin off again. He'd had enough of them taking jabs at one another.

"No. It's been more than five summers since she voluntarily left the pack. I didn't keep tabs on her. I simply let her know she could come back any time she wanted."

"She's not coming back." Rosco was quick to make his position known on even the implication of having Deanna return to the pack of her birth.

"I didn't say she *was*. I was just saying, I'd welcome her back if she wanted to come."

"She's my mate, and heavy with my pups. She's not going anywhere without me."

Quinlin's responding, "oh" was followed by a couple of seconds of silence before he released an expletive.

"Motherfucker..."

From the single word and his intonation, Rosco's spine stiffened in preparation. His fingers curled into fists at his sides. He was certain whatever Quinlin said next was going to piss him off.

"Motherfucker, who?" Rahm asked when Quinlin didn't fill the air with sound quickly enough.

"Barry Thorne. It has to be him. The scent should be fading, but he'd still carry something of Blacktooth on him. Especially if he's had contact with his family. Which is possible because they weren't happy when I kicked his ass out."

Rosco's gaze clashed with Rahm's. He recognized the name. It was Deanna's former mate. She'd only told him the name once, but it was etched into his memory.

"You kicked Deanna's former mate out of the pack and didn't think to warn her?"

He couldn't keep the growl out of his voice and he didn't give a shit if he offended Quinlin. Deanna was most important to Rosco. Failing her, put anyone on his scat list—no matter who it was.

"I'm going to ignore your tone because I know how you CVP fuckers get about your mates. To answer your question. No, I didn't think to contact DK. If you recall, I told you I wasn't keeping tabs on her. I had no idea where she was.

Besides, Barry had another mate after Deanna. He wasn't put out when she set him aside. He was mated again before she left Blacktooth Summit. Why would I think he'd seek her out?"

Rosco, leaned over the phone receiver lying on the desk, wishing he could look Quinlin in the eyes.

"Did you happen to send him away with a nest egg? Or did he leave with whatever he had in his personal accounts with human banks?"

"I said I kicked his ass out. Why would I reward him for being enough of a fuck up that he's not welcome in this pack?"

"What are you thinking, Ros?" Rahm's question was immediately followed by a reply from Trip instead of Rosco.

"He's thinking Mr. Mate Scorned was huddled up with Sally Swift plotting against Deanna and her nest egg."

A burning flame started in Rosco's gut and fanned out, heating his face and causing his wolf to batter against his senses trying to get out. He and the beast were torn between wanting to go to Deanna making sure she was safely within his sight and running the entire thirty miles to Cummings to find and eliminate Barry Thorne.

He couldn't be allowed to breathe the same air as Deanna. The thought alone caused Rosco to nearly lose control of both his man and his beast. He didn't care about the money. He was more than capable of providing for his mate and their offspring.

No. What had him fighting not to behave in the most primal way was the thought of Thorne occupying space within sight of Deanna. Her pained expression when she told Rosco about the many heatless summers she'd spent with Thorne and how he'd berated her for not giving him progeny, was fresh in Rosco's mind. If Thorne had been within sniffing range, Rosco would gladly rip out his throat so he wouldn't be able to use his windpipe and vocal cords to say another word—let alone berate someone for his own failings.

Quinlin's question cut across Rosco's spiraling internal conflict between the two parts of himself.

"Who's Sally?"

Rosco couldn't speak. Controlling his beast and maintaining the barrier he managed to erect to keep Deanna from feeling the depth of his emotions was taking all he had. Thankfully, he didn't have to expend mental energy to explain anything to Quinlin.

Normally, CVP business stayed within the pack. However, these were special circumstances. Having their two disgruntled members being seen together in heavy discussion, made them allies. At least temporarily. So Rahm filled the Blacktooth pack alpha in on the issues following Rosco's mating with Deanna.

"I need to know who we're dealing with here. Why was this Thorne kicked out of your pack?"

To Rosco, Rahm's voice sounded as if it was coming from very far away. He heard him, but it felt as if the alpha was whispering to him from across the bridge instead of the desk separating them.

"We don't tolerate wolves who abuse their mates." Quinlin's reply was thick with disdain.

"He abused Deanna and you're just now kicking him out?"

Brody's voice held a steely quality, and his gaze heated the side of Rosco's head before he turned to receive it.

"Now, you wait a fucking minute, Bear. He never abused Deanna. If he did, she never told me about it. If she had, he would've been the one to leave instead of her.

It was his mate after her. She went to her mother and they came to me. I saw the evidence before it healed. After I beat his ass, I put him and all of his shit on the border of our land and told him don't come back."

Finally, Rosco was able to marshal his feelings enough to speak. "You're wrong."

"I'm wrong about what?" Quinlin's question came quickly.

"He did abuse Deanna. He just didn't use his fists with her."

Quinlin's curses came before him admonishing himself aloud for missing the signs and not pressing her to tell him more when she came to him about breaking her mate bond with Thorne.

"I knew in my gut there was more to it than the rumors of him catting around on her and her not wanting to hold him back, because she couldn't give him pups. I should've listened to myself."

Rosco didn't join Quinlin in kicking his own ass. If things had gone differently, maybe he wouldn't have met Deanna. Or...they would've met sooner. Like when he'd visited Blacktooth Summit all those moons ago. But, all things happen in the goddess's time. They were together now and expecting their first pups.

After Quinlin was done blaming himself, he gave them more insight into Barry Thorne and the excuses he used as to why he'd failed to be a good partner to not just one mate, but two. He'd finally figured out he was the problem preventing him from having his own progeny.

Sterility was rare amongst shifters, but Thorne was one of those rarities. Once his second mate failed to heat in their many summers together, it became apparent—at least to her. She expressed something Deanna had never dared and suggested he was the source of the problem.

Rosco considered the possibility that Deanna blaming herself was the only thing keeping the coward from trying the same with her. Knowing he hadn't caused her physical harm wouldn't save his wretched life if he so much as sniffed in Deanna's direction.

Their call with Quinlin continued for a little longer, then ended. Before they parted ways, Rahm pulled Rosco to the side.

"Ros, I know that look. I can't say I wouldn't be thinking the same if my Beloved was potentially threatened. So, I won't tell you what you can't do. What I will say, is you need to talk to your mate first.

I saw you in there. Even if you were blocking your mental ass off, she felt some of the fury clearly written across your face and in your body language. You need to talk to her first.

She deserves to know what's going on. It's the best way to keep her safe. Besides. Take it from me, it's impossible to keep a secret from your fatal mate. It's better to give in now than feel her hurt and disappointment with you shutting her out."

Knowing his alpha was right didn't make Rosco look forward to having such a conversation with his mate. With her getting heavier with their pups, he didn't want her to worry—about anything. Especially not her former mate popping up out of the blue with ill intent.

Chapter Seventeen

Deanna tried to focus on the smiling faces of the younglings as they worked diligently on their individual craft projects for the Winter Solstice Festival. Normally, it wasn't difficult, because it was truly a joy for her to work with them. Even more so now that there wasn't the longing inside her which was present for many summers.

Her long-held hope of one day having her own pups was drawing nearer to becoming a reality. She was reminded of it frequently when one of the twins decided to stand their little feet on her bladder or press their tiny palms against the wall of her womb. During those times, she gazed in wonder at the miniature handprint on her abdomen.

Today... at least the past hour, it had been difficult for her to give the younglings her normal level of enthusiasm for their artistic attempts. It started when Rosco reached out over their link to ask her where she was, and it grew from there. She'd felt a hint of his concern but also noticed it didn't fade once she assured him she was fine.

The hint had grown into something else over the course of the hour and she became more uneasy. Not even the sweet, joyful faces of some of CVP's youngest pack members could mute the feelings. Something was definitely going on with her mate.

Her distraction wasn't due to feeling his unease, but in the deep-seated feeling he'd actively erected a barrier between them. He was doing it again. The same thing he'd done when he'd gone to the council meeting without her. Only this time, he wasn't as effective. Deanna feared it wasn't for lack of trying.

She didn't try to shield him from the feelings which ensued as a result of her deductions. Although she doubted if he'd notice.

"DK, are you alright?"

Breena interrupted Deanna's brooding thoughts about Rosco and what he was potentially hiding from her. Pasting a pleasant expression on her face, Deanna was happy only one member of the Greywolf clan could read her thoughts and emotions.

"Yes, I'm fine. Just lost in my thoughts."

"Do you need to sit? You look a little flushed."

Deanna allowed herself to be guided by the hand Breena placed on her shoulder. Sitting in the chair she was offered, Deanna kept her gaze trained on the younglings just in case one of them needed her. It was doubtful they would and probably a good thing they didn't—with her mind being as attuned to her mate as it was.

"Thank you, Breena. But, I'm fine really."

"Sister, you should never play poker. You aren't very good at hiding your hand."

Breena took the seat next to her, propping her chin on her open palm. The chocolate eyes, she inherited from her father, peered at Deanna as if she was attempting to siphon the thoughts from Deanna's head. Despite them not sharing the same eyes, Breena's expression was eerily similar to the one Rosco wore when he already knew what Deanna was thinking and was simply waiting for her to say it aloud or through their link.

Sisterly closeness was something Deanna hadn't experienced in many summers. Lack of tight familial bonds was part of the reason it was so easy for her to leave Blacktooth Summit to strike out on her own. She was sorely out of practice and it showed. Shifter nosiness aside, Breena was persistent. So, Deanna relented.

Knowing they were still likely to be overheard, she spoke to Breena in the quietest voice she could manage.

"Fine. I'll talk. But not here. Can you drive me home?"

"Sure."

Gesturing to one of the other volunteers, Deanna made her excuses for their early departure, grabbed her coat from the hook and attempted to exit the building. Of course, they didn't get away without a few of the younglings stopping her to proudly show off their completed projects. Displaying patience she didn't feel, Deanna gave them each her attention before finally being allowed to continue.

Once they were inside the confines of the vehicle, Breena didn't start the engine immediately. Instead, she turned to Deanna.

"Okay, I can drive you home, but do I need to get mama along the way?"

"No! No. That's not necessary, Breena. Let's not bring your parents into this. It could be nothing."

"DK, you didn't see your face. It's definitely something."

Deanna knew her mate bond with Rosco was strong, but she had no idea facets of it were so visible to others to the point her emotions were on display to such a degree.

"I'm just..."

Trailing off, she glanced out the window at the other buildings along the primary road leading in and out of pack town center. Breena didn't prod. She simply started the car and began to drive. Deanna's wolf nudged against her mind. She was as agitated as Deanna that Rosco had seemingly blocked them out.

Although their beasts didn't or couldn't talk directly to one another, unless they were shifted, her wolf felt the loss of connection as well.

We must go to our mate. We must go now!

Yes, wolf. I know.

"Something is going on with Rosco." Deanna yielded to her wolf's demands. Turning as much as her belly would allow, she stared at Breena earnestly.

"I need to speak to him. Face-to-Face. Can you take me to the Alpha house instead?"

"Sure. I don't want to pry into your mating, but you said something was going on with my brother. Is he okay?"

Deanna wouldn't lie. She could tell enough to know Rosco wasn't injured, but physical injury wasn't the only kind possible.

"He's...something. He's not physically hurt, but I need to see him."

Her request was all Breena needed to hear. Expertly maneuvering the vehicle, she increased her speed. Unlike amongst humans, there weren't speed limit signs alongside the roads. Had they been there, Breena would've definitely violated the posted limits.

As they drew near to the Alpha house, they noticed Brody climbing into his pickup. By the time Breena had parked in the semi-circular drive, a large transport truck slowly rolled from one side of the house. As it passed, she saw Trip was the driver. She hadn't interacted with him much. But, seeing him leaving in a trailer truck wasn't unusual.

Deanna's senses told her Rosco was still there mere moments before she heard his voice in her head.

"Mate? Why are you here? I thought you were helping with the younglings?"

Deanna's response was simple and without guile.

"I'm here for you, Rosco."

By the time she'd opened the car door and turned to get out, he was within sight. Rushing to her side, he was there before she had both feet on solid ground. With his hands at her expanded waist, he practically lifted her from the seat.

The feelings Rosco had attempted to shield her from came pouring in when she was standing in front of him. The force of them caused her to sway and hold tighter to Rosco's arm. It put her wolf on even higher alert than before.

"You're so angry...What happened?" A sliver of anxiety was present in the sensations she received from him, but the anger dominated. So, she addressed it first.

His facial expression and the tension in his shoulders said he didn't want to tell her. However, his desire was overruled by the strength of their bond.

"Thorne has been seen in Cummings."

"Thorne?" Deanna's brow furrowed as she searched Rosco's eyes for the answer she didn't want to believe. *"Thorne? As in Barry Thorne?"*

"Yes."

DARIE MCCOY

"Why would Barry be in Cummings? And why would him being there make you so angry? I'm long over him, Rosco, and I'm not afraid of him. He can't hurt me anymore."

*"Knowing he **did** hurt you is enough for me to be angry."*

Stepping as close to him as her protruding belly allowed, Deanna slid her hands up his chest until they rested on his shoulders.

"I appreciate your desire to defend me, but you don't need to avenge my past hurts. My happiness. Now. Here. With you. That's the best revenge."

"No. It's not. Besides, him being in Cummings isn't the whole story. He was with Sally. They were talking and having lunch in the diner."

The line between Deanna's eyebrows deepened. She felt somewhat as if her cognitive skills were slipping with her stunned, one-word questions. *"Sally? How would Barry know Sally? And what would they have to talk about?"*

"I don't know how they are acquainted, but there is only one logical answer to your second question. You."

The bottom of Deanna's stomach dropped. Nothing about her former mate being in Cummings made sense. Moons ago, she'd previously thought she'd seen him there. But she'd brushed it off. As far as she knew, Barry was living his happily mated life in Blacktooth Summit with the she-wolf who could give him the progeny he so coveted.

"Trust me. I'm the last thing on Barry's mind. He had his new mate before I ever left."

"Come with me, Mate. There's so much more than you know."

Deanna reflexively leaned into Rosco's side as he guided her away from the car and toward the little bridge leading to their home. Only Breena calling out to them reminded Deanna of her presence.

"Yeah...So, I guess I'll see you two. Glad to know you're okay, big brother."

Too concerned with Rosco's serious countenance, Deanna barely spared Breena a glance when she remembered to express her thanks. Rosco managed to do a little better, but not by much. They made the walk back across the creek in silence. However, the millisecond they crossed the threshold and the door clicked closed behind Rosco, Deanna looked to him for an explanation.

"What is it that I don't know? Is it the reason you blocked me out earlier? Again?"

To his credit, Rosco wore his shame on his face and transmitted it through their link. The feeling carried more weight than the anxious anger he'd been trying to mask.

Guiding her to the sofa in the main sitting room, Rosco relayed his morning starting with Trip's arrival and ending after the phone call with Quinlin. Even during the retelling, Deanna noted how difficult it was for Rosco to maintain his composure. He was furious. His protective instincts were in overdrive and she could tell all he wanted to do was hunt.

Her mate wanted to take the fight directly to the perceived threat and eliminate it. Deanna's wolf was one hundred percent on board with him laying waste to any threat to their family, but Deanna was also processing the information she'd been given.

She'd known from the moment she went into mating heat with Rosco the issue of her heat not triggering with Barry wasn't her fault. It was him. While they weren't one hundred percent animals, shifters carried many similarities. One of which was the innate ability to recognize and preserve themselves. Nature had complete control over their reproductive capabilities.

And nature had prevented Deanna from going into heat with a mate incapable of seeding her to produce a pup. She'd never seen it first hand, but Deanna had heard about female shifters going into heat when their males were away. They'd nearly gone mad before their mates returned to ease them through the heat cycle.

Remembering how she felt during her own experience, Deanna couldn't imagine the insatiable drive to procreate without being able to assuage it. She'd wanted to crawl into Rosco's skin to get relief. The goddess had spared her life and sanity by holding the process at bay until she was mated to a shifter who possessed what was necessary to complete the cycle.

Once her thoughts were racing a little less, Deanna was able to pick at some of the other details Rosco mentioned.

"Don't be mad at Quinlin. It's not his fault I never told him about Barry."

Slipping her hands into Rosco's she tangled their fingers together, keeping him from fisting his. The set of his jaw combined with the low vibration of his anger conveyed his thoughts clearly.

"I'm serious. The Deanna I was, when I went to Quinlin for permission to set my mate aside, was the bravest I'd ever been. And even then, I wasn't brave enough to be vulnerable. I was too cowardly to tell him the rest of things when it came to why I wanted to break the bond with Barry.

As much confidence as I had in him as my alpha, I played to the thing most males seemed to be obsessed with as my primary reason. Even after Quinlin took my side when I told him about Barry wanting to add a third to our mating to bear his offspring, I didn't trust him enough to tell him about the verbal abuse.

It appears the young she-wolf he mated after me, is much braver than I was. She recognized that she was worth more than a mate who blamed her for his issues."

"Mate, I won't listen to anyone speak poorly of you. Even you." Rosco's steel gray eyes blazed with a different fire when he cradled the side of her face in one of his large hands.

"You were not a coward. What you did took the kind of strength most shifters never have to display. We mate for life. Even when the matings aren't fatal. They are still for life.

For a she-wolf, without the support of her family, and in the face of being abused, to even speak to the Alpha took courage. But to actually follow through...took rare mettle. I'm proud of you."

Unexpected emotion swelled inside Deanna as she listened to Rosco. His reassurance meant far more than he could imagine. Leaning into his touch, she closed her eyes allowing the feeling of his unwavering acceptance and support to wash over her.

With the hand still holding hers, Rosco moved their linked digits to her rounded belly. His gaze held hers captive as he stroked his thumb along the bump.

"If you weren't brave, you would've stayed at Blacktooth Summit. You wouldn't have left to explore the continent, nor discovered the confidence in yourself to pursue purchasing your own business. If you hadn't done those things, we might not have met. Then we wouldn't be here to share this moment... In our home. With our pups growing inside you.

So, I can't let you speak of my mate not being the bravest shifter I've ever met. Because it would be a lie."

As if they were in agreement, the pups became active inside Deanna's womb. When she looked down at her stomach, she gasped as the two little hand shaped outlines appeared. They were far enough apart for it to be clear one was from each pup.

With quiet reverence, Rosco traced each impression with his fingertip. Whispering quietly to them, he accepted their agreement with his assertion of their mother being brave and strong. The moment brought the tears hovering at the corners of Deanna's eyes, streaming down her cheeks in rivulets.

It was then that she also understood the undercurrent of anxiety she'd felt from Rosco. This. Moments like this were potentially being threatened. She hoped there was nothing to Sally and Barry appearing to join forces. However, it was doubtful. Either way, she was with her mate. No one would be allowed to jeopardize what they were building together. No one.

Chapter Eighteen

Rosco had always considered himself a patient shifter. Despite the reputation wolves had for being violent and impulsive, he hadn't ever been one to fly off the handle. It was part of the reason Rahm had selected him as beta from a pool of well qualified shifters with more summers under their belts.

However, it was taking every ounce of control he had to refrain from letting his beast take over. Allowing it to run free. But doing so would mean leaving his mate's side. With the knowledge of a potential threat to her and their pups, him seeking out the danger to eliminate it wasn't an option. Not if it meant he would leave her in someone else's care.

While he trusted his pack mates and security team, he couldn't put Deanna's protection in anyone else's hands. It wasn't an option. Introspection wasn't required for him to understand why he felt that way. Even if they weren't fatal mates, Rosco was certain losing Deanna would be the end of him. He wouldn't survive a second mate and pup being taken from him.

So, instead of giving over to his primal instincts, Rosco stayed with his mate day and night over the next few days. The rotation of security in Cummings didn't report any further sightings of Thorne and Sally.

Which could mean they'd parted ways, but likely meant they were taking great care to not be seen together.

It was on the morning of the fourth day, and Deanna was showing signs of irritation at having him so closely monitoring her movements.

"Big Bad..."

Deanna dragged out the shortened version of the nickname she'd given him. The whole name was Big Bad Wolf. When she was feeling playful, it became BB. He didn't need a cipher to figure out she'd grown tired of her restricted schedule.

Padding through the connecting door between their bedroom into the nursery, she held a stack of tiny clothing in her hands. When Rosco went to relieve her of the small load, she pulled the garments close to her chest.

"I've got it. They aren't heavy. Although I don't know why I'm bothering. If these pups behave anything like the alpha cubs or the younglings I've dealt with in the past, clothing isn't going to be worn often. It almost feels like a waste to have this stuff."

Rosco smiled at her observation. "Can you blame them? It's the chance to be mobile and explore versus being barely able to roll over on your own. I'd choose naked shifted freedom too."

Deanna shook her head, but her smile peeked out. "It would serve them right if I had some of those little outfits made like I've seen humans put on their pets."

Placing the stack in the top drawer beneath the changing station, she tapped her chin. "Come to think of it, that's not a bad idea. That way, there won't be any need to chase them down to get them clothed."

Shaking his head, Rosco tugged her into his arms. "Kitty Kat, we are *not* dressing our pups like human pets."

Plucking at the buttons on his shirt, Deanna poked out her bottom lip.

"But it would make our lives so much easier. They make them with openings for their tails and everything."

"Mate—"

Rosco cut off his reply when he heard the phone ring. The fine hair on the back of his neck rose. Setting Deanna away from him, he headed toward the door.

"Stay here. I'll get it."

Taking the stairs two at a time, it was still ringing when he reached his office. Snatching the phone from the base on his desk, he practically barked into the receiver.

"Rosco."

"Ros, you need to get down here."

Trip's voice wasn't the one Rosco had expected to hear when he picked up the phone.

"Down where? And what's going on?"

"I'm at the office, and Sally just strolled in here with that wolf I told you about. They've asked to see Rahm, and Sally is asserting her rights as a pack member to call an emergency council meeting."

The growl rumbled in Rosco's chest. He'd known it was going to be something, but he hadn't expected this. What could she possibly think to gain by calling an emergency council meeting?

"I'll be there shortly."

It was a miracle from the goddess he didn't break the device when he slammed the phone back onto the receiver. He lifted his gaze to see Deanna framed in the doorway.

"What's happened?"

As much as he wanted to, Rosco didn't attempt to block her from feeling the ire building within him.

"Sally is back. She brought Thorne with her and has requested an emergency council meeting."

"Can she do that?"

Deanna walked fully into the room. Rosco met her halfway, pulling her into his embrace.

"Yes. It's rare, but any pack member with a grievance can request a council meeting. Usually, the emergency meetings are reserved for dire situations or..."

Rosco's voice trailed off as the thought occurred to him. *She wouldn't. Would she?*

"Or what?" Deanna's brow lifted with her question.

"When someone wants to challenge for pack alpha."

Deanna's lips rounded into a perfect 'O' shape as she stared up at him.

"Surely, she doesn't want to challenge Rahm for the position of alpha."

Alpha females weren't unheard of. However, it wasn't likely Sally would dare challenge Rahm herself. Even in her prime, it was unlikely she'd best the bear shifter.

"No. I doubt she'd do it herself."

Leaning slightly away, Deanna stared up at him in disbelief. He was certain the same thought he'd had just seconds prior had occurred to her.

"You don't think Barry will challenge Rahm? Can he even do that? He's not a member of this pack."

"He can if he has the support of at least one pack member. It's a really old rule of the pack. It wasn't even invoked when Rahm challenged Champ."

Setting her a little away from himself, he reached for the phone again.

"Who are you calling?"

"My parents. I'm not leaving you here by yourself."

Deanna's fingers covered his pressing the phone back onto the base.

"No. You're not going anywhere without me."

Rosco's denial was immediate. "Uh-uh. You aren't going anywhere near those assholes, Mate. Absolutely not."

Deanna's head shake matched his, and the set of her chin was just as stubborn.

"If you're going, I'm going. I'm a member of this pack and I'm your mate. Besides, this wouldn't be happening if you hadn't mated with me."

"Are you blaming yourself because those two assholes are doing what assholes do?"

Rosco never thought there would be a day he'd refer to Sally Swift in that way. But he'd also never anticipated her morphing into a being who would slide into insanity simply because the goddess blessed him with a second chance.

Deanna's fingers flexed against his chest, and shook her head again.

"No. I'm not blaming myself for their actions. But there's a clear line between my appearance in your life and the relationship between you and Sally degrading. It's also highly doubtful Barry would ever even set foot in Cummings if he hadn't somehow found out I was here."

Rosco couldn't dispute her argument, but he didn't like it. Not in the least. She was right though. Although he was torn between exposing her to their presence or leaving her home when he wasn't there to personally protect her.

He'd barely nodded his agreement when the phone rang again. Pressing the speaker button instead of lifting the handset, Rosco answered. Trip's voice came over immediately.

"Good. You're still home. No need for you to come this way just yet."

"Why not?"

"They're gone. Apparently Sally Swift isn't the only one who's read the pack by-laws. She forgot she had to allow for a minimum of twenty-four hours for the council to be notified and assembled."

Keeping Deanna close to him, Rosco rubbed her back in light soothing circles. Some of the tension in the room dissipated, but they were both still alert.

"Trip, is she doing what I think she's doing?"

"I think so, but Rahm didn't say."

Rosco wondered why Trip was calling him instead of Rahm. While Rosco was dealing with the death of his first mate, Trip had stepped up, along with Aldis and Jeontugi, to help out by taking on some of Rosco's beta duties. He was unofficially Rahm's third, but didn't really want the title. Still, he'd been called on again when Rosco refused to leave Deanna's side.

"Where is Rahm? Why didn't he call himself?"

"He's still around. He said some shit about me taking it upon myself to call you the first time. So, I could close the loop and let you know to hold off. He's probably still gonna call you though. You know you're his main squeeze. I'm just a side piece."

"Where the hell do you come up with this shit?" With a quick head shake Rosco added. "Never mind. I don't want to know. I'm done."

Without another word between he and the flip talking jaguar shifter, Rosco disconnected the call.

"So, what now?" Deanna met his gaze with a probing stare.

"Now, I'll talk to Rahm to get a first-hand accounting of what happened. Then... we'll see."

Nodding, Deanna settled against him, laying her head on his chest. A nuzzle to her springy curls preceded Rosco resting his chin atop of her head. He interpreted her sigh as contentment, but felt the slight undercurrent of concern interwoven with her relief at the temporary reprieve.

Rosco was certain when the subject arose again, there would be another debate concerning whether she should stay home. As much as he didn't want Thorne breathing the same air as Deanna, Rosco wasn't sure he wanted to win their battle of wills. Her being out of his sight was equally untenable.

～

"You've got to be fucking kidding me." Rosco cocked an eyebrow at Rahm, who was leaning against the sturdy mahogany desk in his home office. "When Trip said Sally asked for an emergency council meeting, I considered the option, but I didn't actually believe she'd pull this shit— let alone find someone dumb enough to follow through with it."

"Well, she did. On both counts."

Rahm's arms were loosely folded across his chest. His posture denoted his lack of fear and more so irritation at the situation.

"So, what do you think of this guy? Of all of this?"

"He's a piece of shit."

"That's a given." Rosco tilted his head to one side with his comment.

"Am I worried he has a chance? No. He's big. Moves like he's been trained in something. But none of it matters to me. I'm not ceding my pack to a coward who likes to lord his strength over those weaker than him. We've had one Champ. I'll be damned if I'm the reason we get another."

Propped against the wall on one shoulder, Rosco's arms were folded across his chest in a similar fashion as Rahm's.

"You know it doesn't have to be you, right? If Sally can invoke archaic pack rules, so can we." Without waiting for Rahm's input, Rosco continued.

"It's true that an alpha can be challenged by anyone with the support of at least one pack member. But the alpha doesn't have to *physically* fight any challenger. They can select a champion."

Standing up straight, he dropped his folded arms. "I'll do it."

Rahm's gruff chuckle couldn't be mistaken for true amusement. "I figured I'd have to fight you to *keep* you from volunteering. I suppose I don't have to remind you alpha challenges tend to be to the death?"

"I have no intention of dying." Rosco's reply was immediate.

Even though he'd been a youngling still in pack primary school when Rahm challenged Champ, he remembered it well. During challenges, every pack member was present—from infants to the elderly. Their future rested on the outcome. So, no one was prevented from witnessing the event.

Alpha challenges tended to be to the death because the loser rarely conceded to living a life having failed to achieve their goal in front of so many eyewitnesses. Champ didn't have a beta to champion his claim to remain alpha. Rahm had Rosco.

But, Rosco's desire to step in had less to do with his role as beta than it did his desire to wipe Barry Thorne from the goddess's green earth. Whatever had possessed him to come in search of Deanna would be the decision he would regret when he gasped his last breath.

"Since you have everything planned out, what do you intend to do about Sally once you've kicked the shit out of the little wolf she sent to do her dirty work?"

Lowering his brows, Rosco stared at him. "I never said I had it all planned out. But, we both know Sally can't stay here. I hate it for Shep, Glenn, and Silas. But, she has something eating her from the inside out. This has gone way beyond grief."

Rahm's chin dipped in a slow nod of agreement. "I'll speak to Glenn—unless you want to do that as well."

He was being baited, but Rosco didn't fall into the trap. However, he knew he was the one who needed to speak to Glenn. He'd been a second father to Rosco. The least he could do was speak to him before it was declared in front of the rest of the pack.

"It's gonna suck ass either way, but I'll talk to Glenn. He probably already knew it was coming."

A buzzing hum cut into anything else they had to say. Starting out low, it grew closer at an alarmingly fast rate. Eventually, the unmistakable thwapping beat created by rotor blades slicing through the air filled the room. Excited shrieks from the cubs echoed through the house as Rosco and Rahm left via the closest door to investigate.

Once they sighted the source of the noise, Rosco understood the twin's excitement. There was a helicopter landing in the clearing beyond the cabin which was once Brody and Portia's home. Walking at a moderate clip, Rosco and Rahm approached the visitors.

They weren't unexpected. However, their mode of transportation was. Once the landing skid was firmly on the ground, the pilot cut the engine. The thwapping beat slowed along with the rotor blades. The doors swung open on both sides and booted feet hit the ground.

A new engine sound replaced the helicopter as Brody's pickup pulled off the road onto the grass. By the time Rosco and Rahm were within ten yards of them, Brody, Quinlin, one of his brothers, and an unnamed wolf were in conversation.

"I suppose driving would've been too normal for you." Brody's dry quip didn't seem to faze Quinlin.

"Driving takes too long. Besides, I was invited. I wasn't asked to use a particular mode of transportation—just as long as I showed up."

With the way they sniped at each other, Rosco wondered how they managed with Quinlin being Brody's commanding officer in the military. The bears in Rahm's family didn't seem keen on taking orders from others.

Waving off Brody's grousing, the Blacktooth Summit alpha introduced himself to Rahm, then proceeded to introduce the rest of his small contingent. As it turned out, the wolf Rosco was unfamiliar with was Thorne's uncle.

Rosco's wolf jumped to attention and he was acutely aware of the older shifter.

"Orion will represent the Thornes."

Almost as tall and broad as Rahm, Orion extended his hand to the alpha in a respectful shake.

"My father has asked me to extend apologies on his behalf. Barry has brought enough shame on the Thornes with his actions. I'm not here to defend him. Only to bear witness."

With a curt nod, Rahm gestured to Rosco. "This is my beta, Rosco. He's also Deanna's mate."

Orion turned nearly black eyes onto Rosco, who met his stare head on. A nod was his only greeting, which Rosco returned. Waving them toward the Alpha house, Rahm laid out his expectations. Neither of them mentioned Rosco would be representing him in the challenge fight.

Chapter Nineteen

"*Mate, it's time.*"

"*Okay. I'll let your mother and sister know.*"

Rosco's voice inside her head gave Deanna a mild start. Setting aside the book she wasn't reading, she stood getting Breena's attention. Rosco's mother was in the kitchen busying herself by baking bread. They'd both come over early that morning to keep her company while Rosco went off to meet with Rahm. After relaying Rosco's message to Breena, Deanna walked into the kitchen.

"*Don't leave until Papa gets there to pick you up. I'm going ahead with Rahm.*"

"*I won't.*"

It had taken a lengthy conversation for Rosco to agree to this arrangement. She was aware and appreciated how seriously he took his role as her protector. However, he also had a duty to Rahm as his beta. An Alpha Challenge had been made. He would be negligent in his duties as beta to be anywhere other than at his alpha's side.

Playing on his sense of honor and duty combined with promises to go nowhere alone were the only way she managed to get him to see reason. That and agreeing to have his mother and Breena come over to babysit her while he spoke with Rahm.

Earlier, they'd heard the distinct sounds of an aircraft.

Looking out of the window, Breena had confirmed a helicopter landed in a clearing near the Alpha house. She didn't recognize the male shifters who exited, but gave very detailed descriptions of them.

"If I weren't happily mated, I might find an excuse to go over there to have a sniff or two. They are all so well-built..."

"But you are mated. So, it does you no good to salivate over other shifters."

Even as she said it, Eileen Greywolf pushed her daughter aside so she could get a glimpse for herself.

"Oh my..." Eileen's hand went to the base of her neck as she leaned closer to the window.

Their antics made Deanna curious as to what they were seeing, so she joined them. When she saw the grouping of males, her breath hitched.

"You know them?" Breena asked excitedly.

Deanna's initial response was a mute nod as she took in Jeffrey and Randall Quinlin standing next to Orion Thorne. Quinlin she expected, but seeing Orion was a surprise.

The summers she'd been gone from Blacktooth Summit hadn't changed either shifter much. They were still just as intimidating looking as they were before. Orion's hair, swept atop his head in a messy bun, seemed to have slightly more gray. But otherwise, he was the same. As were Quinlin and his brother.

When she finally found her voice, Deanna managed a verbal answer to Breena's question.

"Yes. They're from Blacktooth Summit. Jeffrey Quinlin, the alpha is the one with dark hair wearing a blue shirt. The big one next to him is his brother and beta, Randall."

"What about the other one?" Eileen preened as if she needed to be certain she was looking her best.

"Orion. Orion Thorne"

"Thorne?!" Both Eileen and Breena nearly shouted together.

"Yes. He's Barry's uncle."

"Well, why would they bring him here?"

Seeming to forget she was just ogling the newcomers along with her daughter, Eileen put an arm around Deanna's shoulders. The hug warmed Deanna. They both immediately switched gears from appreciating fine male forms to consoling her.

The sound of vehicles cutting their engines pulled Deanna from her thoughts. A short moment later, Jonah Greywolf walked through the door. While Rosco had inherited his mother's eyes, he took everything else from his father.

Jonah Greywolf was a shifter of few words, and his countenance appeared stern. However, his chocolate brown eyes held a kindness which put Deanna at ease. His gaze swept over the three of them before he gave a curt nod.

"Everyone ready to go then?"

"Yes, Papa." Breena answered for the three of them.

With Eileen and Breena on either side of her, they followed Jonah outside to the truck. Rosco's three brothers were in a second vehicle waiting for them. They trailed the truck when Jonah pulled away from the house. None of them spoke for the duration of the ride. Instead of going to pack town center as Deanna expected, Jonah stopped the vehicle at the edge of an open field. There were already others present.

It was apparent some had come on foot, while others had driven. How ever they made it there, it appeared the entire pack was present. Deanna had never experienced an Alpha Challenge. So, she had no idea how the process worked—especially not in the Central Valley Pack, since she hadn't been born there. It seemed even the younglings of holding age were in attendance.

When Jonah cut the engine, more of Rosco's kin were standing beside the truck. Deanna felt like a package insulated by a wrapping of bubbles. She couldn't see anything beyond the broad backs of Rosco's brothers and cousins in front of her. Breena's mate and his family joined the contingent as they moved through the assembly.

Deanna wasn't sure of where they were going until the shifters in front of her created an opening and she saw Rosco standing next to Rahm. Behind them on a raised dais were Mama Ley and Carleeta with the alpha's cubs. Also there were the shifters making up the pack council and the rest of Rahm and Carleeta's family. Off to the side of the dais were Quinlin, Randall and Orion. While Orion's stare was elsewhere, Quinlin and Randall watched her group approach.

Mentally, she felt her wolf pacing inside her. They'd never been in such a large gathering of shifters before. It made both of them anxious. Knowing the purpose for the gathering didn't provide any comfort.

So many shifters. Too many. Too many scents.

I agree, wolf. Far too many.

Deanna's gaze locked onto Rosco's. Her own feelings of anxiety were only mildly tempered by the calming sensations from her mate. Through their link, Rosco's voice was soothing, while his outward appearance was stoic. His eyes were the giveaway, which contradicted the words he pushed into her mind.

"It's going to be okay, Kitty Kat. There's nothing for you to worry about. I promise."

"How can you say that, Rosco? Orion, Quinlin, and Randall are here."

Rosco remained at Rahm's side, but his stare bore into Deanna peeling away even the slightest barrier between them.

"Deanna, you are my mate. You and the pups you carry are my reason for drawing breath. I won't let anything or anyone bring harm to you. Trust me. Trust me and know this day will end with the two of us together. Happy and safe. That's all I ask. No matter what you see. No matter what you hear. Just know I have it under control."

"Wait, Rosco? Why does it sound like you're going to do more than simply stand up as Rahm's beta?"

As Deanna posed the question over their link, a different energy invaded the crowd and a murmuring swept through the assembly. Although it wasn't necessary in order for her to know the source of the change, Deanna swept her gaze around until she landed on the newest arrivals.

Barry strutted through an opening in the crowd with Sally walking slightly behind him on his left. Deanna wished she was surprised to see his youngest brother, Cortland, but she wasn't. He'd always followed Barry around like a lost human pet.

When her former mate's cold stare met hers, Deanna straightened her shoulders, but didn't make any outward acknowledgement of him. Barry was far more transparent. With a glance at her rounded abdomen, he clenched his jaw causing a muscle there to visibly tick. His fists balled at his sides.

"Look at me, Mate."

In a command only she could hear, Rosco demanded her attention. Her response was immediate. For the first time that day, he moved from Rahm's side and came to her. Cradling her face in one hand, he lowered his head, placing a gentle kiss on her lips.

He gave her no other words. But none were necessary. His declaration was clear. When he turned to retake his position next to Rahm, Jonah stood to Deanna's right, slightly in front of her, however not enough to block her view. The Greywolf clan stood together with Rosco's siblings and parents making up the first layer of her shifter cocoon.

Deanna couldn't stop herself from seeking out the Swifts and Carnahans. They weren't near the dais, but they were visible. Glenn and his son Silas stood shoulder to shoulder, while Sally's sister and other relatives were set apart from them along the same line of the circle made by the onlookers in the field.

Rahm's booming voice garnered Deanna's full attention. Clapping his hands to quiet the murmurs, he took control.

"We all know why we are here. A challenge has been made to take my place as alpha of the Central Valley Pack."

A chorus of objections were heard from the shifters present. Raising his hands, Rahm motioned for silence.

"We don't have to like it, but the pack rules are clear. Anyone, shifter or human, can challenge the alpha with the backing of a pack member."

Gesturing toward Barry, he continued, "this wolf, Barry Thorne, formerly of Blacktooth Summit pack, has issued the challenge."

Despite it being obvious who his pack sponsor was, Rahm still asked, "is there a pack member willing to support his challenge?"

Sally stepped forward. Her expression was pinched with defiance. To Deanna, her entire body appeared as one tightly wound bow string. Deanna couldn't imagine the thoughts going through her mind as she stood before her pack members supporting an outsider to oust her alpha. And for what?

Deanna had never met Millie, but everything she heard spoke of a kind shifter with a giving spirit. How could such a being come from a person as bitter and vindictive as Sally? Even Sally was a contradiction to who she was reported to be prior to her daughter's untimely death. So, was this grief? If it was, what could Sally hope to gain from helping Barry become CVP alpha?

Not for a second did Deanna believe he would succeed. She simply wondered what they hoped to achieve. Barry wasn't a leader. Although he'd been trained in fighting styles through the work he did outside of the pack, he'd never even been on the pack security team. He occasionally groused about BTS leadership, but never gave any indication he wanted to be alpha. Yet, here he was, standing in front of the alpha of her new pack. It didn't make sense.

Once she spoke, Sally's voice was clear. She was holding firm to whatever her reasons were to endorse Barry.

"I support him. It's time for a change. We need new leadership."

"Sally, don't do this!"

While it held an undercurrent of steel determination, the pleading note in Glenn's voice was unmistakable. He was making it known before the pack that he wasn't on board with his wife's decision. He had one hand on Silas's shoulder as if reminding Sally of what she had to lose if she continued.

Deanna observed Sally turn away from her husband, her lifemate, giving Rahm her full attention.

"I stand by my word. I am within my rights as a member of this pack."

Nodding, Rahm's face gave nothing away. Since his normal expression resembled a scowl, it was hard to determine if any of this angered him.

"That's correct. You are well within the rules."

Stretching one arm out, Rahm tapped Rosco's shoulder. Once Rosco took a step forward, the pieces fell into place for Deanna. His words from earlier came back to her. This is what he meant.

"Just as you're within your rights as a member, it's my right as alpha to select a champion to face any challengers."

While Deanna wanted to say something, she'd silently agreed to stand by her mate during whatever happened. Internally, her woman was concerned for him. Conversely, her wolf was standing at attention growling encouragement to him. She was particularly blood thirsty when it came to Barry.

Deanna couldn't blame her beast. Her instincts had been suppressed during her mating with him. Being free of him brought her and her wolf closer together. But the beast would never forgive him.

When Rahm released his shoulder, Rosco whipped his shirt off, dropping it at his feet. Barry did the same. Deanna couldn't help but compare the two. Where they were both fit and appeared healthy. Rosco's muscular bulk seemed harder. His entire being gave off the air of his wolf riding close to the surface. Although it was likely her imagination, he seemed to get larger right before her eyes.

Conversely, Barry seemed paler. Next to Rosco, he lacked the edge which would strike fear in an opponent. He nearly matched him in height, but when he exposed his hairless chest, he seemed like more of a pup standing next to a full-grown wolf—despite him being nearly a decade older than Rosco.

"Rules?" Barry flicked his gaze to Rahm, before quickly returning it to Rosco.

Rahm's reply held more than a hint of condescension. "This is an Alpha challenge. You yield or you die. The only rule is that you fight alone."

Barry nodded, then flicked his wrist at Sally and Cortland. The arrogance in the gesture wasn't lost on Deanna.

How did we ever submit to such a weak wolf? Her beast didn't hide her disgust.

I don't know. I can't imagine how we did.

Deanna didn't have long to commiserate with her wolf before Rosco and Barry moved farther into the center of the circle. The move placed them far enough away to not harm anyone else in the fight. Yet they remained close enough for everyone assembled to have a clear view.

When Barry next opened his mouth, he showed that he hadn't grown much in their time apart. If he had, he would've noticed how eager Rosco was to defend his alpha. Deanna felt it through their bond. She sensed her mate's carefully contained fury via their link. Taunting

Rosco would only serve to make his end more painful. But, Barry didn't know that.

"Don't worry, beta. I'll make this quick. I'll also take care of DK. She and I have some unfinished business anyway."

"You would do well to keep my mate's name from passing through your lips. Wipe her from your thoughts completely in these last moments of your life. You might live longer."

"Big talk for a little beta. If you were a wolf worth your salt, you would be alpha of this pack instead of a second. I guess you're only good for knocking up mates, then losing them."

The growl rumbling from Rosco's chest was enough to make the ground beneath their feet tremble. Deanna was watchfully concerned, but, Rosco proved he wasn't so easily manipulated. He didn't pounce as Barry obviously expected. One corner of his mouth tipped into a feral grin.

"You talk too much."

Deanna wasn't sure what she expected to happen following Rosco's statement. But what followed showed her a side of her mate she couldn't fathom existed.

Chapter Twenty

The moment his father drove onto the challenge field, Rosco sensed Deanna's anxiousness. He considered he should've warned her of his plans, but knew foreknowledge wouldn't make her worry any less. As it was, she felt some level of responsibility for what was occurring. Nothing was further from the truth.

Neither of them had control of what was predetermined from the moment they breathed their first breaths. They were fatal mates. Had they gone the rest of their days without knowing one another, they could've survived. However, the depth of connection they had as fatal mates would've been missing. Nothing else compared to it.

And, as much as he loved Millie, Rosco knew the intensity of his union with Deanna surpassed what he had with her. He knew now, it didn't mean he loved Deanna more. It was simply a different bond. One he never could've had with *anyone* else.

As beta, he was supposed to remain by his alpha's side. Yet, he couldn't allow Deanna to continue to worry needlessly. He did what he could to reassure her before returning to his post. The moment Barry Thorne appeared flanked by Sally and another shifter bearing a strong family resemblance, Rosco had to exert additional control to keep himself from tearing across the field and ripping the coward to shreds.

She hid it well, but Rosco felt the change in Deanna when Thorne appeared. He wasn't under the delusion his mate still had feelings for the shifter. However, she'd experienced emotional trauma. At least some of it was bound to resurface when she saw him again—even after more than five summers.

Rosco listened to Rahm go through the formalities of the alpha challenge. He felt a smidgen of sympathy for Glenn as he made a last-ditch effort to get Sally to recant and come to her senses. He could've saved his breath. Rosco observed Sally's posture. There was no talking sense to her.

Any sadness Rosco may have had knowing what would be next for Millie's mother was wiped away when Barry Thorne opened his stupid mouth. He didn't heed Rosco's warning regarding Deanna. No. Thorne kept talking.

When he made mention of Rosco's loss so flippantly, it took considerable effort to keep his beast from pouncing. Because that was exactly what Thorne wanted. All Rosco allowed from his beast was a rumbling growl.

Can we kill him now?

His wolf's anger was tinged with anticipation. Very little brought the beast more joy than maiming in the name of protection. Protecting his mate and defending his alpha were high honors.

After a beat without a response, the beast prodded him again.

*Can we kill him **now**?*

To his beast, Rosco gave an internal nod. Outwardly, Rosco gave his opponent a smile signaling the beginning of the end of his short life. He was done listening to Barry Thorne and only had four words left to say.

"You talk too much."

Barry's stance with his slightly bent knees and his loose fists hinted at some type of fight training, but it wouldn't do him any good. As shifters, they both had increased speed and strength in comparison to humans.

In complete contradiction to what one would expect in a fight, Rosco advanced on Barry with his hands down at his sides. He didn't throw a punch or attempt to grab the other shifter in any way. His steps were measured and purposeful.

Obviously thinking he'd been given a gift, Barry threw the first punch, presenting Rosco with exactly what he wanted. A limb to break. Accepting the offering, Rosco stepped through in a motion which flipped Barry onto the packed earth while Rosco still held onto Barry's arm.

Shifters are made sturdy. So, even at the awkward angle, Barry's arm was still mostly intact. That is until Rosco placed a foot on Barry's chest and pulled. His grip slipped, but not before he felt Barry's arm slip out of socket at the shoulder.

With a pained yell, Barry rolled away and sprang to his feet. His right arm hung limply at his side. Shuffling steps backed him away from Rosco as his pain-filled eyes searched around wildly. There were no flip words or cruel reminders dropping from his mouth—only heaving breaths. Rosco could practically see his thoughts racing.

I thought we were going to kill him. His beast prompted him impatiently.

We are. But first, he needs to suffer and know that no one will come to save him.

To his credit, though Rosco didn't want to give him any, Barry didn't yield. It was obvious he was outmatched, but he held up his left hand defensively. Slowly, Rosco allowed his wolf's claws to descend. Shifting wasn't against the rules and the appearance of Rosco's claws seemed to remind Barry he was a wolf as well.

Probably thinking to accelerate his healing, he shifted into his wolf form. Rosco wasn't fazed by the confidence Barry gained in his shifted body. The warning growls and snapping jaws did nothing to stop his approach. Shifting had done the work of mending Barry's arm.

He launched himself at Rosco, swiping at him. The malice gleaming in his eyes didn't compare to the promise of destruction in Rosco's. This time, it was a paw Rosco grabbed, sinking his claws through the layers of fur into the muscle. When he struck bone, the yelp Barry released lacked the threatening timbre of the growls he issued moments before.

Jerking, Rosco pulled, this time severing ligaments leaving the bone protruding at an odd angle. While he denied his wolf a full shifting, Rosco allowed the beast everything else. It was what they both wanted.

He paid no mind to the blood spurting from the wounds he caused to the other wolf, as he ripped Barry apart. When he lay before Rosco broken but still bleeding, he shifted back into his humanoid form.

Barry was beaten. He knew it. Rosco knew it. Yet, he used his last breaths to spew his twisted logic, blaming Deanna for turning his pack against him. A red veil descended over Rosco's vision. Leaning over Barry, Rosco bared his teeth.

"Didn't I tell you not to let my mate's name cross your lips again?"

It was a question which didn't require an answer. Grabbing the arm closest to him, Rosco finished the job of removing it completely from Barry's body. Using it as a club, Rosco proceeded to beat him into unconsciousness, with his own limb.

Barry's chest rose and fell with shallow breaths when Rosco dropped the limp arm on top of him. His beast wasn't satisfied. Barry still breathing the same air as their mate couldn't be allowed. Giving his beast what he craved, Rosco shifted.

By the time his wolf yielded back control, Barry was nothing more than a pile of body parts and Rahm was calling his name to bring him back from the edge.

The wildness of his beast kept Rosco's breathing labored for a few moments after he returned to his humanoid form. None of the blood splattered on him belonged to him. Barry hadn't managed so much as a scratch.

He felt nothing for the pile of Barry leaking into the earth. Nothing at all. The fury Rosco had directed toward him had faded into dullness. The only thing keeping him tethered to reality was the infusion of caring and loving sensations he received from Deanna through their link. His gaze searched out hers.

Looking past where Rahm stood in front of the dais, he found her eyes waiting for his. The strength of her feelings shining brightly in their depths. His feet automatically took him to her as if no one but the two of them existed.

"Don't you fucking dare!"

Rosco's steps faltered at his mother's thundering declaration. Swinging his attention to her face, he realized she wasn't speaking to him. What happened next seemed to occur in slow motion, but was likely mere seconds.

His mother bounded from Deanna's side shifting into her wolf in the span of a breath, leaving her clothes in a tattered heap. Whirling completely around, Rosco made certain his mate was safely behind him.

Before him, his mother, in her wolf form was snarling and snapping at Sally, who stumbled, backing away.

"It's not fair!" The pain in her declaration was coated in bitterness. "Why couldn't it have been him? Why does he get to live when she doesn't?!"

Deanna's soft hand closed around his, offering Rosco an emotional lifeline as Sally unraveled before their eyes.

"My Millie was kind and loving. She didn't deserve not to grow old. She should've gotten to be a mother to her pup and a grandmother."

Swiping at the tears on her face, she sniffled, staring at the grass beneath her feet. When she looked up again, the hatred she directed at Deanna was palpable. It was so strong Rosco was tempted to tuck his mate behind him. Blocking her view of Sally's venomous stare.

His mother remained between Rosco and Sally, but she was soon joined by Mama Ley, who remained unshifted. However, she wasn't wearing her normal bright smile. The scowl was reminiscent of her son's. So, she obviously wasn't planning on giving Sally one of her signature hugs.

"Sally, you've said enough. More than enough." Her voice carried a quiet authority.

Unfortunately, Sally was too far gone to hear her. As far as Sally was concerned, Rosco couldn't be more of a disappointment. Millie was a sweet mate. He loved her dearly. Her death had robbed them both of a future with the family they created. He'd always miss her. However, the goddess had seen fit to gift him with another opportunity to be a mate and a father.

He didn't seek it out. And despite his turmoil during the early stages of their mating, he wouldn't turn away from Deanna and his pups. Not only was he physically incapable of doing it, he had no desire to. Yet, it seemed as if him not mating with Deanna was exactly what Sally expected. That he would honor Millie by never being happy with another. By never loving and being loved again.

She continued to rant about the unfairness of losing her only daughter and her first grandpup.

"Then he," she pointed to Rosco, "went and gave her my Millie's life! Now she's big with his pups, living in the Beta house and getting everything my Millie will never have."

Forgetting herself, Sally took a step toward Rosco and Deanna, only to have his mother block her path with a snarling growl. Shooting the wolf a glare, Sally stopped in her tracks.

"Sally, you seem to think you're the only one who suffered when Millie died." Mama Ley looked behind Sally. "What of your mate? He lost his only daughter and first grandpup as well. Your sons lost their only sister. And Rosco…" She glanced over her shoulder at him, "lost his mate *and* his pup."

Taking a step toward Sally, she shook her head. "It's okay for you to grieve and be hurt by the loss. What's not okay is for you to take it and turn it against Rosco, Deanna and the rest of this pack. What you have done here today cannot be forgiven."

Tilting her chin defiantly, Sally looked past Mama Ley to the dais.

"Being Alpha Mother doesn't mean you speak for the pack. You're not the alpha. You can't kick me out. I was born into this pack. The Carnahans were here long before Champ traded for you and brought you here."

Sally's reference to the way Mama Ley came to be mated to Champ was low. No one ever spoke of it for a reason. The mating wasn't a love match. It was a negotiation between two alphas for the life of a young female shifter with few options.

Hearing more movement from the dais, Rosco turned to see Carleeta standing from her seat, adjusting the cub in her arms. Walking down the few steps, she stopped in front of Deanna. Echo and Lei-Lei followed silently. Without a word, she extended the youngling to Deanna and looked down at the twins.

"You two stay here with Miss DK."

Without another word to them, she went to stand next to Mama Ley. During the entire exchange with Sally, Rahm remained silent.

However, when Carleeta stepped from the dais, he moved to stand behind her. He didn't speak and the next words came from Carleeta.

"Mama Ley is Alpha Mother. But you're right, Sally. She's not the alpha. But I am. As Alpha Bitch, I *can* speak for the pack. And I stand by my mother's words. What you have done here, bringing this disgraced wolf into our pack to challenge my mate, it cannot and will not be forgiven."

Taking a step forward, until she was standing shoulder to shoulder with Mama Ley, Carleeta spread her hands.

"Now, you can either leave on your own power, or we will *help* you leave."

Sally's face paled and her mouth dropped open. Whipping her head around the crowd, she seemed to be searching for someone to come to her defense. Rosco watched as she finally made eye contact with Glenn. The older man's eyes were sad with his obvious disappointment. When he and their son turned, giving Sally their backs, a low murmur went through the crowd. With their silent statement made, Sally looked to the Carnahans. The murmurs were peppered with gasps when they collectively did the same as Glenn and Silas. They all turned their backs refusing to acknowledge her silent pleas.

Tension and sadness blanketed the area. Seemingly aware of the intensity, not one youngling cried out or even asked questions. With the exception of her family, all eyes were on Sally.

Breaking the silence, Rahm finally spoke.

"What is your decision, Sally Swift? Will you leave on your own? Or will you require... assistance?"

The tears which pooled in Sally's eyes following her family's rejection, spilled down her now splotchy cheeks.

"I know my rights, Rahm Monteparse. You can't do this without the consent of the council."

Sally was grasping at straws. She'd already been before the council with a warning. Yet, she continued to—or at least she attempted to refer to them for aid. After her bid to get the pack council involved, each word she attempted was drowned out by a snarling growl from his mother.

"You can't do this! I'm a member of this pack!"

"Maybe you should've thought of your ties to this pack before you swindled that idiot into challenging my son."

In all of Rosco's thirty-eight summers, he'd only seen Mama Ley's bear three times. The fourth occurred this day. When she shifted, Carleeta's lioness quickly followed. Rosco watched in amazement as the female shifters lined up behind Carleeta, his mother and Mama Ley.

Sally's expression went from belligerent to stricken. Her slow, backwards steps faltered over uneven parts of the ground as she started edging away. For each step she took back the pack of female shifters moved forward.

Rosco guessed she'd realized her family would be of no help because she no longer looked to them as she was herded from the field. In an unwise and sudden show of aggression, she bared her teeth. Even though she hadn't shifted, her hackles were raised when she released a snarl of her own.

Faster than he'd ever seen her move, Rosco watched in awe as his mother lunged forward swiping at Sally, ripping her shirt from her body and knocking her to the ground. In a fur flying flurry, they tumbled around before Sally, in her coyote form, managed to wiggle away. Streaking southward, the coyote ran from the field with the group of females hot on her trail.

Rahm took over in the aftermath of the challenge, assigning shifters to tasks to set the area back in order. With all of the attention following the challenge being focused on Sally, Barry's brother had slipped away.

"Don't worry about him. I'll get his ass. Blacktooth will handle our shit." Quinlin's response to the news was no less than Rosco expected from the no-nonsense alpha.

No objection came from Barry's uncle, who was standing at the edge of the dais facing the direction the females had chased Sally. Rosco wasn't the only one who noticed the wolf's fixation.

"Orion? Orion?!" Quinlin finally got his attention.

"Yeah?" Orion's gruff reply sounded as if he was on the verge of ripping into his alpha for interrupting his gazing into the distance.

"Since you're here representing the Thornes, it's on you to tell your Pa about Cortland and anyone else who's sympathetic to Barry. It's time for them to choose."

Orion's only answer was a curt nod before he went back to his vigil. Rosco only briefly considered what had Orion's unwavering interest before giving his full attention to his mate.

While the pack members were dispersing and stopping by to voice their support of Rahm and Rosco, she'd quietly taken a seat on the stairs leading onto the dais. She held little Saddiq in her arms as Lei-Lei and Echo played in the grass at her feet.

The image was a glimpse into his possible future and Rosco was struck by how utterly thankful he was the goddess saw fit to lead them to each other. They had both been given the opportunity to share in the rare phenomena of finding one's fatal mate. The connection surpassed the sentiment of love, but that feeling welled inside Rosco as well when he observed her with the younglings while her belly was round with his pups.

The link between them was almost tangible in its intensity. Deanna glanced up as if she felt his gaze. Her expression was filled with tenderness, and adoration poured through their bond. Walking over to her slowly, he squatted until they were eye level.

"Are you okay, Kitty Kat?"

He stretched out a hand to stroke her hair and noticed it was still covered in Barry's blood, so he dropped it, clasping both between his bent knees.

"I'm okay, Big Bad. Are you?"

Still holding Saddiq in one arm, she performed the motion he'd halted, stroking his hair from his forehead then cradling one side of his face. Closing his eyes, he leaned into the feeling of her soft touch.

"I have never been better, my love."

Chapter Twenty-One

Deanna stood at the center of the nursery surveying the final results. Her gaze dwelled on the baby bed they'd been gifted from Carleeta. She'd made it especially to accommodate twins. Having twins of her own, and being a skilled carpenter helped her craft something which could grow with the pups until they were old enough to sleep independently.

She'd also made them bassinets that could be connected or separated if necessary. Deanna and Rosco had decided not to learn the sex of the pups. So, the room was decorated in soft colors to soothe the little ones without leaning toward any particular gender color combination. It didn't matter to Deanna anyway.

During her time living among humans, she had learned a lot about their preferences on such matters, but she was simply happy to be blessed with pups of her own. Which is why knowing if they were female or male wasn't a priority. They would be loved just as deeply either way.

Rosco's strong arms encircled her and the scruff from his beard lightly abraded her skin when he kissed then nuzzled the crook of her neck.

"How are you feeling, Kitty Kat?"

"Like I have two over-ripe melons taking turns pressing against my internal organs sending me to the bathroom at a moment's notice and making my back ache from the weight."

"I'm sorry, I'll have a talk with them about tumbling on your bladder. But, in the meantime..."

Positioning his large hands beneath her distended abdomen, Rosco lifted. The ache and pressure in her lower back lessened. Deanna wasn't sure if she wanted to kiss him, climb him or both. The relief was nearly orgasmic. She had no idea how much she needed it.

Rosco continued to nuzzle her neck, peppering her with kisses and murmurs of appreciation and encouragement. The combination of the affection, his proximity and the praise had the effect she should've been able to predict. Deanna's core pulsed lightly.

In the final stages of her pregnancy, her desire for her mate had reached a level near what she'd experienced during mating heat. Sometimes, all she had to do was smell him nearby and she was ready to pounce on him. Deanna needn't say anything to Rosco. His sharp inhale and the arousal she sensed through their bond conveyed his knowledge of her situation.

Her mate was always ready and willing to satisfy the urges when they arose. Within seconds they were in their bedroom, she was stripped naked and settled in the nest of pillows while Rosco was behind her feeding his length into her dripping center inch by delicious inch.

"It's okay, Kitty Kat. I'll take care of you."

His deep voice in her ear while the scruff of his beard grazed her neck and shoulders, ratcheted her desire up even further. His tender words, speaking of taking care of her stimulated her in ways she wouldn't have imagined.

As he gently pumped inside her, they alternated between speaking to one another via their link and aloud, exchanging words of love. No matter how much she asked, he refused to be as rough as he was prior to her being so large with the pups. However, lack of robustness didn't mean unsatisfying.

The delectable stretch of her walls to accept his girth was almost enough to send her into release before he'd done more than deliver a few thrusts. Deanna held on, although she knew if she'd tipped into orgasm before him, Rosco would simply get her there again when he reached his peak.

With one hand on her sensitive breast, and the other at her hip keeping her positioned for his invasion, he plucked, twisted and gently pinched her turgid peak. The sensations were so overwhelming, Deanna wasn't able to process them before her body was unceremoniously tossed into nirvana. It was explosive, coating his cock in her essence. Rosco's grunts became growls as he attempted to control himself while hurtling toward his own release.

"Fuck, Kitty Kat. Your pussy is so hot. I can't—oh! Fuck-fuck-fuck-fuck!"

Rosco's appreciation was capped off with feral rumbles from deep within his chest as his seed shot from his shaft. Despite it being impossible for it to take root, her channel milked his length for every drop of his cream.

Soft kisses to the back of her neck soothed Deanna as she came down from bliss. Cocooned in her mate's arms, the gravity of how her life had changed in such a short time hit her. But instead of weighing her down, she felt buoyed—as if she were floating to her highest high.

After the Alpha Challenge, and Sally was literally run out of the pack, things changed for Deanna. For the better. While no one had been openly hostile and many had accepted her, there were apparently those with conflicted loyalties not just to Sally, but to the Carnahans.

Glenn and Silas had always made it clear they accepted Deanna as Rosco's mate and treated her kindly. However, the Carnahans were distant. They weren't overtly rude. They simply didn't show themselves friendly. Following the challenge, it appeared they had a change of heart. Deanna wouldn't say any of them were her best friends, but they'd made it clear where they stood when they showed Sally their backs that fateful day.

As things changed for her within the pack, things also improved in her relationship with her mate. Their bond as fatal mates was beyond anything Deanna had ever experienced. Yet, hearing Rosco refer to her as his love added a layer she didn't know she wanted. Their connection was already so strong by then, she'd thought the words of love unnecessary. She couldn't have been more wrong.

Hearing him say it, was a form of healing she hadn't anticipated, for both of them. It pulled them from the shadow of their previous matings to stand firmly together. Rosco eliminating a threat against their mating and their pack freed them both. Their lives and their love were reclaimed and given freely to one another.

~

"Uh-uh. No. I don't want to."

Deanna shook her head vigorously. A sheen of sweat covered her body, plastering strands of hair to her neck and face. Her new mother, Eileen, had been kind and attentive, sweeping Deanna's hair atop her head in a bun to keep it out of the way.

She had provided whatever Doc Portia and Mama Ley said was needed whenever Deanna needed it. None of those things meant Deanna was open to the gentle words Eileen spoke. She didn't want to do this anymore. The pain was too great.

"Come on, Sweetheart," Eileen coaxed as Deanna held onto Rosco, who was holding her as upright as the searing pain would allow.

In the gift which kept giving, he received a portion of her pain due to their mate link. So, his sweat had nothing to do with the temperature of the room and everything to do with him attempting to manage his discomfort while doing what he could to comfort Deanna through the delivery of their pups.

Mama Ley's firm voice broke through Deanna's fog, and she knew she would have to yield.

"Rosco, get your mate over to the birthing stool. Whether she's ready or not, those pups are coming. Using the stool will help things move along and give her the support she needs."

Even through the haze of her pain, Deanna sensed his apology before he sent the words via their link as he lifted her in his arms.

"I'm sorry, Kitty Kat. We have to listen to our elders. They've been here before. They are just trying to help."

Striding across the room, he stopped next to the crescent shaped birthing stool. Carleeta had brought it and some other items over to assist Deanna in a safe delivery, as comfortably as possible.

Once he placed her on her feet in front of it, Rosco positioned himself behind it and helped her lower herself on to the seat. His bare chest pressed against her back skin to skin adding to the feelings of comfort and support. Not sure if she had any fight left in her, Deanna grabbed the handles jutting out from the sides.

A short while later, they welcomed the first of their pups into the world. A little she-wolf who shifted almost immediately after her first cry rent the air. On the heels of the first, less than five minutes in fact, the second pup made her appearance. Daughters. The goddess had blessed Deanna and Rosco with two beautiful daughters.

Once she'd expelled the after birth and the birthing corner had been set to rights, Mama Ley, Doc Portia, and Eileen left them alone to bond. Other family and friends were gathered downstairs waiting for an opportunity to welcome the newest pack members.

Deanna leaned against Rosco's warm body, holding both infants to her chest while Rosco's strong arms encircled them all. His head was buried into the crook of her neck. So caught up in her own feelings, it took Deanna a moment to realize the wetness on her neck wasn't from their sweat. It was from tears. Her mate's silent tears dripped onto her skin and rolled down her collarbone into the fine hairs on one of their daughter's heads.

Deanna felt the depth of his emotions via their bond, so she knew they weren't an expression of sadness. No. They were from a joy so heartfelt the only way to release it was through weeping. At the same time, he gently swayed, rocking all three of them in his arms.

Eventually, he lifted his head raining kisses on her shoulder, neck and the side of her face. His fingertips ghosted across the tops of their daughters' little peach fuzz hair as he spoke in a reverent whisper over their link.

"Thank you, my love. It feels like I should say more. Something flowery to express myself. You've given me a gift I'd given up hope I'd ever have. Yet, the only words I have to convey my feelings are 'thank you'. It seems wholly inadequate, but it is all I have other than to say I love you more than I dreamed was ever possible. And... I'm thankful to the goddess sending you on the journey which led you to me and for making Rahm force me into a vacation leading me to you. I don't want to imagine a

world where I didn't get to feel the completeness which comes from loving and being loved by you."

Deanna's heart turned to mush at Rosco's declaration. Words failed her and despite what he'd thought when he started, he *did* have flowery words to give her—and he delivered an entire field full of them, imprinting his feelings on her heart.

"I love you, Rosco Greywolf. I love you and these pups who grew in my womb from the seed you planted. The goddess has blessed us both beyond measure. Now, it's up to us to live each day basking in those blessings."

They sat quietly enclosed in their bubble, soaking up one another's love for a while before a soft knock came to their bedroom door.

"Is it okay if we come in?"

Rosco's mother made the request, but Deanna heard the shuffling and additional breaths before she ever spoke. No words were needed between Deanna and Rosco to acknowledge one another's feelings. Rosco called out to them.

"Yes, it's okay."

The pups stirred against Deanna's chest, but their eyes remained closed. Apparently, kicking their way into the world and their early shifting, wore them out. They'd nursed a little before dropping into slumber in her arms.

His parents, all three of his brothers, Breena and her mate, Donovan, entered the room. Eileen was the first to approach the bed. Her smile was in her eyes, making them sparkle. With hands clasped to her chest, she gazed at the babies as if she hadn't been in the room a short while ago when they arrived.

"We won't stay long, but we wanted to see you. We'll have to announce their names to the pack. Since you two didn't want to have advanced knowledge of the sex, I'm hoping that doesn't mean you didn't have names picked out."

A soft smile tugged the corners of Deanna's lips upward. Looking over her shoulder at her mate, she nodded for him to do the honors.

"Yes, we have names." Touching each in turn he introduced their children to their family.

"This is, Arianna Zoe." The baby wiggled under her father's light touch and her bottom lip disappeared into her mouth, but she didn't open her eyes.

"And this, is Lillianna Paige. We'll call them Ari and Lilly."

They'd considered naming one of the twins Millie to honor Rosco's first mate, but decided against it, because they didn't want her to have to live up to anyone else's legacy. However, the shortened version was a nod to the shifter who held a special place in her mate's life without her completely shouldering the mantle.

"Those are lovely names. We'll let the others know. You two take as much time as you need."

After a short visit, they left under a hail of blown kisses from Eileen and Breena. Rosco and Deanna remained in their blissful bubble for a moment longer, bonding with their children. CVP had a tradition Deanna hadn't grown up with in Blacktooth Summit.

The newest pack members were presented to family, the alpha and a select group when they were born. Later, when they were a little older, they were brought before the entire pack to accept their rightful place as members. Based on what Deanna was told, they would still be too young to fully comprehend what was going on. So, it was more for the pack to have the opportunity to express their commitment to welcoming them into the CVP family and contributing positively to their upbringing.

Deanna was overcome with sentiment when she looked into the faces of everyone who gathered in their home to welcome their children into the world. Although none of them were bound to her by blood, they had become her family.

Warmth covered her as her mate drew her into his side. He held Ari in the crook of one arm while using the other to pull Deanna and Lilly close. Both pups had opened their eyes, the same stormy gray as their father's, staring at those in their limited view.

Deanna looked from them to the smiling faces of everyone gathered in the large sitting area, and her heart was filled with joy. A joy she and her mate both thought was lost to them, had been reclaimed.

Epilogue

Deanna's smile was so wide, Rosco wondered if her cheeks ached. There was no feeling like knowing his mate was so happy and unashamed of showing it. Their pups frolicked in their modified dresses looking extremely adorable—although Rosco was loath to admit it.

Folding under the sweet coercion of his mate, Rosco had relented in his position on having clothing made which could accommodate the children in whichever form they chose. Shifter children grew fast, so it wouldn't be long before it wasn't an option. But for now, on this beautiful spring day, they worked.

Their little tails peeked from beneath the ruffled edges of their dresses as they tussled on the grass with Rahm and Carleeta's youngest cub, Saddiq along with Tasi, Brody and Doc Portia's cub. As much as Saddiq had taken many of his mother's genes, he was a bear shifter like his father as was Tasi, who took more than the form of her beast from her father. She was a feminine, miniature version of the grumpy bear.

The younglings were enjoying themselves as Deanna, Breena and Marigold watched over them. The massive yard at the Alpha house had once again been transformed for Brody and Doc Portia's wedding. To Rosco, it looked like a fairy tale had been plucked from one of the books he read to his daughters. The arch under which they'd recited their vows was overflowing with lush greenery and vibrant flowers.

The tables and chairs were set atop a low wooden platform installed specifically for the occasion. The center of each table held colorful bouquets of flowers in vases. Like he'd thought earlier, it looked like a fairy tale image come to life.

He turned his gaze back to his mate, marveling at the way the spring sunshine reflected beautifully off her golden-brown skin. Without thought, he licked his lips, remembering how all that lovely skin tasted on his tongue.

"If I didn't know you were already mated to Deanna, I would say you were a wolf ready to make his mate claim. But since you have, I'll just suggest you look for a babysitter tonight. I do *not* volunteer."

Rosco cut Trip a dark glance. "As if I'd ask you to look after my pups. You barely keep yourself alive."

Trip had the audacity to look offended. "I'm not the one who had to be forced into taking a vacation, but whatever you have to tell yourself about me to make you feel better."

Trip folded his arms across his chest. Like Rosco, he'd been coerced into more formal attire for the occasion. Thankfully, the weather was mild enough for the garments to not cause them to sweat profusely.

"Of course no one had to force you to take vacation. You disappear once a month to go somewhere that you don't tell anyone about. You get plenty of time away."

Something foreign flashed across Trip's face before it shifted into his normal irreverent expression. Although Rosco saw it, he decided not to mention it. A shifter was entitled to keep some of their thoughts to themselves.

They bantered for a few moments more before Trip wandered away and Rosco walked closer to his family. As he did, he swept his gaze around, taking in the other revelers present for Doc Portia and Brody's wedding. A tall, bronze skinned man stood next to the doc and her parents. He'd been introduced as her older brother, Yancy.

Until then, Rosco hadn't been aware the doc had any siblings. It was just the three of them talking until Brody joined them. Rosco couldn't say he recalled Brody smiling so much. Although Rosco had spent more time with him in his bear form, even prior to the issue he had on his mission, Brody wasn't a big talker, nor did he give off cheerfulness.

When he reached his mate, Rosco wondered again about something that had been on his mind since the girls were born. Being at an actual wedding instead of a mating celebration brought it to the forefront of his mind again. While they'd both been mated before, of the two of them, Rosco was the only one who'd gone through a wedding ceremony as well.

He didn't want Deanna not to have all the experiences she desired. And, he also wanted to be tied to her in all the ways he could be. Since she walked in the human world by owning the Inn, it was possible she'd developed an appreciation for some of their customs. Coming to a stop next to where she was seated, watching the pups and cubs, he leaned down to kiss her upturned lips.

"Hey, Big Bad. You decided to take a break from giving Trip h-e-double hockey sticks?"

"Mate, where did you learn that, and why are you spelling?"

Deanna's smile was so big and her cheeks lifted so high, it caused her to look like her eyes were closed.

"I did live among humans for many summers. And I'm spelling, because I don't want to use bad words in front of the younglings."

Her gaze darted to the balls of fur tussling, yipping and playing in the grass. He started to tell her it was unlikely they knew what she was talking about, but caught himself. The Alpha cubs were talking now and they'd taken to repeating most of what was said around them like, they were little macaw shifters instead of lion and bear cubs.

So, instead of giving his mate guff about it, he simply nodded before pulling a chair closer and sitting next to her. Arranging his seat so that his legs bracketed her chair on either side, he leaned over to nuzzle the sweet spot on her neck. Ignoring the audience of Breena and Marigold, he yielded to temptation giving her skin a little lick and a nip. Giggling, Deanna lifted her shoulder, but didn't move away.

"What are you up to, BB?"

"I thought it was obvious, Kitty Kat."

Deanna's head tilted as she melted into his affectionate nibbling.

"Hmm... You may have to state it clearly."

Sliding his fingers into her hair, he fisted them, tugging at the curly strands.

"I'm up to taking you across the bridge and fucking you in every single room of the house. We have to practice for your next heat cycle."

"Mmm. I'm all for the practice, but the goddess can do me the favor of holding off on another heat cycle—at least for a few summers."

"Whatever you want, my love. Extra practice it is."

A nod to his sister was all it required to secure a youngling sitter, before he tugged Deanna to her feet. The guests of honor were so wrapped up in each other at that point, they didn't stop to say goodbye. Their steps didn't even falter when they encountered Mama Ley wrapped in a pair of strong arms, entangled in a very heated kiss.

No, Rosco was determined to keep his word to his mate. So intent on it, he lifted Deanna into his arms and sprinted the remaining distance to their home. If the rest of his days were like this one, the goddess would never hear one complaint from him.

The End

Let's Keep in Touch!

Want to be in the know about what I'm doing and what's next in my writing journey? Sign up for my monthly newsletter to receive inside information, sneak peaks and excerpts before anyone else.

https://sendfox.com/DarieMcCoy

Is the inside view from a newsletter not enough? To get more, you should join my Patreon or Ream Stories. Tiers start as low as $5 per month. Dependent on your subscription level, you'll receive many perks from reading along as I write, up to receiving customized book boxes.

https://patreon.com/DarieMcCoy

https://reamstories.com/dariemccoy

Acknowledgments

I was a bit apprehensive when I first started this book. I actually had to stop writing for a little bit and come back to it. Which is why the release date was later than I originally projected. That being said, I love Rosco and Deanna. They've lived in my head since before I wrote Healed (Portia and Brody's story). But, I knew I needed time before I could bring them to the page.

I'm thankful to my tribe of author friends who listen to me wax poetic about my characters and volunteer to be Beta and ARC readers for me every time. Y'all are the best. Brianna and Niccoyan, thank you for being the first to see my words and give me honest feedback. Y'all are the best writing partners ever!

My sincere thanks to my ARC readers. And a special thanks to the social media influencers who keep saying yes when I pop up in their inbox to offer them an ARC. Y'all make my heart smile.

To my Darlings, Delights, Decadents and Divas, all of you give me reasons to keep writing and I sincerely appreciate you. Thank you so much for rocking with me! And last but not least, thank you to the readers who've been with me since day one and keep reading no matter which tangent my muse takes me on.

About the Author

Darie McCoy is an award winning, best selling independent author of contemporary, interracial, romantic suspense, fantasy and paranormal/shifter romance books. A reader first, she enjoys reading books across many genres although romance holds a special place in her heart. Her experience working in a STEM field offers her a unique perspective which she uses in each story she pens.

When she doesn't have her nose in a book or her fingers on the keyboard, Darie enjoys working in her vegetable garden. A serial hobbyist, she also enjoys knitting, sewing, baking and canning. One of her favorite treats to make is salted caramel popcorn. Amongst her friends, she's known to transport the sweet treat in large quantities to share whenever they get together.

Born and raised in the south, Darie stands by the staunchly held southern sentiments that the best tea is sweet tea and college football is life.

Also by Darie McCoy

Central Valley Pack Series

Chosen

Healed

Frost Family Series

For Real

Sano's Queen (A Novella)

Christmas Candy

Draft Pick Series

Draft Pick Season I: Carver

Draft Pick Season II: Andrei

Draft Pick Season III: Denzel (Kindle Vella)

Other books/stories

Involuntary

Just Kiss Me (Part of Cupid's Kiss Anthology)

Toad: Sin City MC Oakland

Controlled Desire: Fall of Desire

The Glassmaker's Helper: The Getaway Chronicles

Tangled Reverence: Preacher's Kid Series

Excerpt

Want to know how it all began? Keep reading for an excerpt from Book One in the series, Chosen.

Prologue

"You need a mate." Rosco's gravelly voice scraped over Rahm's ears with the unsolicited statement that he didn't bother to cloak as advice.

"The fuck I do."

Rahm popped up from his semi-reclined position in the chair behind his desk. Booted feet that were propped on the heavy oak surface, slammed to the floor with a thundering clomp.

"Rahm..."

"Don't start the disappointed beta shit with me Ros. I don't need a mate. This pack is strong and thriving now. And you know who led us there? Me. Without a mate. I fixed most of the shit Champ did in less than one generation."

"I know you did, Rahm. Champ was a piss poor alpha when it came to the day-to-day pack business and his ego drove away valuable members, but he did do one thing right. He mated with a strong Alpha Bitch. She's the reason you exist."

Rosco's gaze was piercing as he reminded Rahm of the one good thing his sperm donor did as alpha of the Central Valley pack.

Before Champlain 'Champ' Monteparse took over the reins from the previous alpha, whom he bested in a challenge that resulted in the death of the physically weaker shifter, the Central Valley pack, commonly referred to as the CVP, was one of the largest and most powerful packs in the Northern Hemisphere. After only ten years under Champ's leadership, the pack numbers had dwindled to almost half and its coffers well on the way to being empty.

The only reason the pack wasn't completely destitute was due to Champ being smart enough to negotiate with the Pacific Coastal pack alpha for the hand of his only daughter, Rahm's mother.

His mother not only came with a dowry, but the knowledge, business acumen and a genuine soul which drew others to her. She's the reason so many pack members didn't leave. A fierce warrior in her own right, she was the one who trained Rahm to take over the role of alpha.

Unlike some packs, the CVP didn't believe in birthright claim to being alpha. Each alpha must earn the title through challenge. Knowing this, Champ stopped spending significant time with Rahm and allowing him to tag along on training exercises when it became obvious that the cub was quickly exceeding him in intelligence, would grow to tower over him physically and eclipse his impressive strength.

Intellect, physical prowess and size were all genetic gifts given to Rahm by his mother. A tall, thickly built woman, the males in her family tended to be larger than normal shifters—even for bears.

Non-shifting bears tended to live in isolation, but the Pacific shifters lived in a manner usually found in wolves—pack style. Champ was smart enough to gain Rahm's mother as his mate, but not smart enough to realize that the father's genes weren't always the determining factor for what animal form a shifter would take.

Instead of taking the same form as his sire, Rahm took his mother's bear genes with very little of Champ's characteristics—*thank the goddess.*

"Did my mama put you up to this? She's been on me about having cubs or pups for years. I can't stop by the diner for five minutes without her finding a way to mention how much she longs to see her family line continue before she moves on to the next realm."

"No. She didn't have to say anything to me for me to know what I know. I see you every day and I'm telling you that you need a mate."

"Tell me, oh wise beta of mine. If I decided to take a mate, who would I mate with? I've fixed a lot of Champ's fuck-ups, but we still don't have good relationships with strong packs willing to let go of their females still able to breed."

"Why would you look outside of the pack? We've grown. There are at least thirty unmated females of age right on pack lands."

"A pack female! What kind of sick perv do you think I am? There's not an unmated pack female that I'm not either related to or that I wasn't present at the birth the day she was born... AS PART OF MY ALPHA DUTIES!" Rahm's horror at Rosco's suggestion dripped from his voice.

At only twenty summers, Rahm had bested Champ in the Alpha Challenge and took over the pack. Which meant he was a minimum of twenty years older than any eligible female in the pack. Shifters are blessed by the goddess with long life spans, so Rahm's forty-four summers was still considered young by shifter standards.

"Rahm, it's not that bad. I know for a fact that Jim has two daughters of mating age that would jump at the chance to have you court them."

"First, who the fuck still says 'court?'" Second, no offense to Jim, but his daughters are dumber than a box of rocks with letters written on them to help 'em make words. That oldest one tried baking me a cake, but didn't realize she actually had to turn the oven **on** for it to get hot enough to actually bake in it."

Starting from his forehead, Rosco ran one large hand down his darkly tanned, weather-worn face. He wasn't fooling anyone. It was obvious that he was stifling a laugh because he knew Rahm was right. Jim's girls were the female version of the idiot twins from one of the Alpha Mother's old books about falling down rabbit holes.

"Ok, Rahm. You win. I'll stop with the mate talk. You're a full-grown bear, you know your own mind. I stand by my assessment though. Whether or not you believe it or will admit it, you need a mate."

Raising his hands in surrender, he rose from the over-sized chair situated on the opposite side of the large dark oak desk. Slapping his cap against his thigh, he huffed.

"I guess I'll go on down by the Richardson spread. Old Man Richardson's wife promised Millie some of that butter she makes and I told my sweet mate I'd get it on my way home today."

"That sounds good. You can save me a trip. The old man was complaining about trespassers. I was actually going to head that way before you came by and started all this mate talk. Take a look around. If anything makes your hair stand up, give me a shout and I'll come out."

"Yes, Alpha. As you wish, Alpha." Saluting as if he was a soldier, Rosco sauntered to the door.

"Get out you cheeky fucker."

Rosco's laughter lingered in the room as he left closing the door softly behind him. Shaking his head, Rahm picked up the phone to call Old Man Richardson to let him know Rosco would be coming in his stead. After a quick exchange with the old mountain lion shifter, his mind forced him back to the conversation he'd just had with his beta.

Kiss my ass. I don't need a fucking mate.

Chapter One

Carleeta wiped the sweat from her brow with a plaid covered forearm. *It's hot as hell out here.* It was late spring and it already felt like summer. Looking down from her perch on the peak of what would become the roof of the house once they finished attaching the plywood to the frame, she watched her crewmates moving around on the ground.

Checking her harness, she moved to the next position and waited for the new guy to pass up another section. Less than four feet away, another member of the six-person crew was also waiting. They worked in teams at each stage. First on the ground, then framing, roofing and finishing. Their crew typically didn't stick around for much of the inside finishing work.

"Hey, Carl! Heads up!" Wall-eye called out in advance of the next piece being passed up.

"Wall-eye...If I have to tell you one more time not to call me Carl, you're going to find out what the rubber on my boots tastes like." There was always one guy who thought it was funny to shorten her name to a masculine form as if to further emphasize what they considered her lack of femininity.

They could all kiss the broad side of her plus-sized ass. It's not like she didn't know who she was and what she looked like. They outed themselves as insecure when they expressed that they thought her physical size made her less of a woman.

Standing at six-feet two in her sock feet, Carleeta towered over most men she met. Couple that with being a long-time member of the over two hundred club, she knew weaker men were intimidated by her size. *Sucks to be them.* Raised in what her bestie called a family of giants, she was confident in who she was as a person. The approval of some insecure little man-boy, wasn't even a blip on her radar.

Shane, her crew partner, stifled his laugh at her threat to Wall-eye, whose real name was Wallace, but one look at his face and you knew why he carried the nickname Wall-eye. He bore an unfortunate resemblance to a walleye fish. She wasn't sure who tagged him with the nickname, but it stuck and he even went so far as to use it introduce himself.

Looking like that and he has the audacity to think I care what he thinks of how I look? Worry about yourself fish-boy. Carleeta kept her thoughts about Wall-eye's appearance to herself. But, if he kept up with this bullshit, she wouldn't hold back. She learned not too long after she started working on a crew that construction was hard on the body, but for a woman, it could be harder mentally than physically.

If the men found a woman on the team attractive, she expended far too much energy making sure it was clear the attraction wasn't mutual but doing so in a way that wouldn't result in a cut harness or some other *accident* on the job. If they took the route of Wall-Eye, they tried to make a woman so miserable that she'd quit. That wasn't going to happen either.

Carleeta had done her time as a journeyman carpenter and after finding a good mentor was finally a master carpenter. She worked on the construction crew, but her other source of income was as a finisher who did custom carpentry work, be it cabinets or furniture. Making enough with her business, she could quit working on a crew anytime she wanted and be okay financially. Carpentry was her passion.

Thankfully, today's threat to Wall-Eye was enough to get him back in line. It was either her threat or the pointed look from the job-boss that made him clamp his trap shut and just work for the remainder of the day.

Having worked in the heat with crushing humidity, Carleeta's sweat-drenched clothing clung to her body accentuating the curves she didn't try to hide, but also didn't dress in such a way as to call attention to them while she was on the job. Unbuttoning the plaid overshirt, she allowed the light breeze to whip the tails of the shirt and cool her torso.

It seemed counter-productive to wear a long-sleeved shirt in the heat, but her father had taught her that it was actually better and cooler to put a loose-fitting light weight long-sleeved shirt on over a fitted t-shirt. The fitted tee absorbed the sweat and if the day wasn't a complete scorcher, the outer layer would keep the sun from burning her mahogany brown skin.

When Ronald made the call to knock off for the day, the relief was evident from everyone. Carleeta had an image in her mind of a long bubble bath. There were some essential oils she'd discovered at the farmer's market that were supposed to be great for sore muscles and today was a great day to test their effectiveness.

"Hey CJ, are you coming out tonight?" Shane knocked the wood dust and dirt from the bottom of his cooler as he looked at her expectantly. It was pay day Friday, which meant the crew would meet up with some of the guys from other crews at a local bar, have a few beers and blow some extra cash betting on the pool games in the back or sporting events on the two big screen TV's on opposite sides of the bar they frequented.

"Aaahhh..." She hesitated in answering, because of course she didn't want to go. She rarely spent non-work time with the crew. Not that she didn't like them. She really didn't care for crowds.

"Aw, come on CJ. You hardly ever come out with us. You have to come at least for a little while. Did you forget we agreed to take Marco out to celebrate his girl agreeing to get hitched to his ugly mug?"

"Hey man! I'm right here. I can hear you." Marco's offended voice cut into the conversation. "Anyway CJ, pay no attention to Shane. Everyone knows he hasn't been the same since his last girlfriend slid into my DM's. He's just lucky I'm not that kind of guy and I turned her down."

"In your dreams Marco. No woman with access to all this, would ever settle for a young'un barely off his mama's tit." With his chest poked out and his arms folded across it, displaying his large forearms, Shane looked Marco up and down and flicked his gaze back to Carleeta, dismissing the younger man.

"Come on CJ. We're meeting at Five Miles at eight o'clock. Just come by for a few minutes. You're a part of the crew, it wouldn't be a real celebration without all of us there. Even Ronald is coming."

The mention of their reclusive crew boss was the thing that let Carleeta know there was no getting out of this *'peopling'* opportunity. She at least joined them on occasion. Ronald never came out with the crew. This would be a first, but it's possible he couldn't find a way to decline either, Marco was the first unmarried member of their crew to get engaged since they all began working together.

Ronald and Shane were already married, the rest of the crew was single. Marco taking the plunge would put their small crew at half and half—single to married ratio. She had no doubts, after hearing about yet another person in her circle getting married, her mother would start up again about Carleeta letting her eggs go to waste.

Her mother was under the impression that Carleeta should be grasping on to any man who was interested in her and begin producing grandbabies before her poor eggs turned to dust. She was sincerely happy for Marco. Sheila was a good woman and he was lucky to have her, but she could almost hear her mother's voice in her ears. She was actually surprised she hadn't called already. Sheila's mother attended the same church, so it was a given that the word was out as soon as Marco dropped to one knee.

Shaking off the feeling of impending doom at the thought of her mother's admonitions and having to actually socialize, she gathered her belongings and resigned herself to a significantly shorter rest period and no long bubble bath tonight as she reluctantly agreed to join the guys at the bar.

~

After his conversation with Rosco, Rahm was antsy and unsettled. When his beta called to relay what he learned on his visit to Old Man Richardson, he let Rosco know he was taking off for a few days. It wasn't often that he left pack lands for any length of time, but the itch below his skin needed to be scratched and he couldn't scratch it here. Having a capable beta allowed him times such as these when he could have brief getaways with the knowledge that his pack would be protected and cared for in his absence.

After driving for a few hours, he pulled his extended cab pickup truck into the parking lot of a restaurant attached to a bar. Adjacent to the bar, across the large lot, was a motel that didn't look too run-down. He made a mental note to check it out after he grabbed a bite to eat.

He'd hit the road without any definite plans; he just filled his tank with fuel and started to drive. That in itself was strange for him, because if he liked anything, it was a plan. But, the itch under his skin had turned into a tug. That tug didn't allow him to turn his truck east as was his usual practice. Instead, he drove south.

Searching amongst the cars, he found a space big enough for his truck. It was a bit toward the back, but it was out of the way which was what he liked. Turning off the engine, he sat for a moment watching the area and scoping out the establishment.

The building, in the distance, had the look of an over-sized ranch house. Were it not for the name, *Five Miles South*, emblazoned above the entrance in neon lights, it could easily be mistaken for the main house of a large ranch. Stretching end to end and around the sides was a large porch with benches spaced randomly against the wall. None were occupied at the moment, but they had the look of being used regularly.

While there was a steady stream of people entering and exiting, it couldn't be said that it was crowded. That's good. He also noticed that there were no children amongst the patrons. A glance at the display on his dash and he understood why there were no children. It was close to nine p.m. on a Friday night. These people were probably out on dates or some such nonsense.

Rahm didn't date. He found the whole process a pointless exercise. He knew he'd eventually have to settle on a mate, but exactly how that would be accomplished, he couldn't say. He had no patience for the games and small talk that went hand in hand with courtships. ***Did people still call it courting?***

Who the fuck knew? Anyway, when he wanted to fuck, he fucked.

No relationships, no mushy feelings or claiming—just fucking. And never on pack lands. He had a couple of places a few hours east of his lands where he went to find a woman willing to satiate his sexual appetite.

His interactions with females, outside of his duties as alpha, were relegated to essentially fuck buddies. Of which, even that list was short. He didn't go back to the same woman more than twice, because despite agreeing to the terms, they still got attached. Even the ones who claimed not to want to be tied down themselves.

Shaking the unwanted dating and mating thoughts from his head, he stepped out of the vehicle and started the short trek toward the bar. Now that he was outside, he could scent the people around him. The vast majority were human, but he did catch slight shifter scents. They were very faint, but they were there.

Keen eyes searched faces and catalogued body language as he tried to match the scents with the owners. It's possible the shifters he scented were latent and living their lives as a human. He'd seen that often enough in his travels. Shifters and humans remained largely separated despite humans not being as superstitious and bigoted as they were in the previous two centuries.

Entering the sturdy, wood framed building, he stopped at the hostess' station as directed by the sign immediately inside the door. The redhead with overly large breasts and big doe eyes was behind the podium that served as the hostess' station.

"Good evening, sir. Will you be dining with us this evening or visiting the bar?" She asked the question, which was probably standard, in such a way that it also sounded like an invitation to do a different kind of *dining.*

"I'm grabbing a bite, but I'll order something at the bar." His gruff tone didn't lend itself to reciprocating her flirtation. She wasn't his type. Besides being much too young for his tastes, the only large thing on her were those over-sized knockers. He'd found women like that couldn't handle all that he had to give, so he didn't waste his time.

Instead of directing him to the bar, the pint-sized ginger flipped her hair over one shoulder, stepped from behind the little stand and moved closer to him in what he guessed was supposed to be a sensual movement, but actually looked like an exaggerated wiggle of her non-existent hips and ass.

"Are you sure there's not anything else I can get you? I'd be happy to show you to one of our best tables. It has a great view." She said as she leaned slightly forward to display even more of her ample cleavage.

"Nope. I know what I want, and I don't want a table—no matter what the view looks like." Tossing her a look of complete disinterest, he stepped around her and strode toward the bar area located on the right-hand side of the building.

He heard the squeak and huff as he left her standing there, but he didn't spare her another glance. She wasn't important and he didn't have the time nor the inclination to placate her. He didn't miss the heads turning to track his progress through the place. He saw them, but acknowledged no one. He was used to the attention.

When he was on pack lands, it was usually because of his station as alpha. Among humans, the looks ranged from awe at his sheer size and lustfulness when their eyes landed on the package no pants he'd found could conceal. Ignoring people, while simultaneously being aware of them, was a skill he'd mastered long ago. He gave them no more of his consideration than necessary. He was on a mission to get a nice rare steak, a potato and the strongest lager they had on tap.

Thank the goddess the bartender was more concerned about doing his job than he was about flirting with the large, brooding shifter seated at the end of the bar with nothing but the wall at his back. He took Rahm's order and delivered the chosen beer mere seconds after the request was made.

In short order, the much-anticipated steak arrived still piping hot. He'd opted for potato wedges instead of a baked potato and after one taste, he was glad that he did. They were hot, crispy and flavorful. They were a great pairing with the steak that had a slightly crisp outside and tender, delicious interior. *I'm a potato connoisseur. Sue me.*

He was lifting a bite of the succulent meat to his lips when the most delectable scent hit his nose. Dropping the food tipped fork to the plate with a clatter, he lifted his head, his eyes scanning the room looking for the source of said scent. His search stopped when his gaze landed on what had to be a goddess in the flesh standing just inside the entrance, peering into the bar area. His beast sat up inside him and forced him to tip his head back to take a larger whiff.

Her scent was...mouthwatering was the only word that could come close to describing it. Not the flowery perfumes that humans doused themselves in, but an earthy feminine musk with undertones that promised the sweetest of treats nestled in the valley of her thighs.

Ours!

The word rumbled through his head so loudly, he wouldn't have been surprised if the whole place didn't go silent—stunned by the volume and conviction of the single roared word.

He knew only he heard the voice. He and his beast were totally in sync ninety percent of the time. This was a ten percent moment. He wanted her. **Fact**. No doubt that he wanted to bury himself for endless hours between those lush thighs. But... His beast was ***claiming***; he wanted far more than a quick dalliance.

Gulping the flood of fluids collecting in his mouth, Rahm watched as she moved closer. So captivated by her, he almost missed the other note present in her scent. *Pack*. Her scent held the slightest hint of the woodsy bouquet all members of the CVP carried in their personal fragrance.

She couldn't possibly be pack though. He didn't know her and there's no way he'd ever forget meeting her. Besides, even-though he scented her across a crowded restaurant, he smelled the human in her. She was at minimum half, if not more than half human.

Human. Rahm wouldn't say he hated humans, but they weren't his favorite of the goddess's creatures—though they did serve a purpose on occasion.

His nose was good. Actually, it was excellent. He could usually identify a shifter's beast from scent alone. Not with her. The only thing he learned from inhaling her natural perfume was something that almost knocked his big ass off the bar stool. Whatever she was. Whoever she was. She was ***his***.

His eyes raked over her, taking in her form from head to toe; cataloging every single detail. She was no petite little miss. He'd guess she stood at just over six feet tall. Even if she took off the low-heeled boots she was wearing, she'd still tower over most people.

The weather was unseasonably cool outside, so she had a light jacket draped around her shoulders. It only served to cover her arms, but couldn't hide the curves of her voluptuous frame. Drawn as if by a beacon, his eyes traveled from her booted feet, to her thick legs, to her rounded hips and small waist before landing on the sumptuous globes exposed by the deep vee neck of the shirt she wore. Her dark brown skin carried a golden undertone.

Her breasts were so abundant, it appeared the slightest movement might cause them to spill from the confines of the form fitting garment. Those were the breast he'd feast on while he fucked her. The breasts his cubs would suckle to gain nourishment to grow. His beast growled in his head, urging him to go to her and claim her. ***Now!***

Shut up beast!

No! Mine! Ours! Claim!

Since when can't you talk in full sentences?

Mate!

Listen you big bastard. We're surrounded by humans. We can't just grab the woman and mate her right here!

Mate!

Hey! Cut that shit out! I wanna fuck her too, but we aren't among pack. We have to do this like the damn humans. Now, shut up and let me think.

To calm his beast and get him to stop thinking of throwing their mate to the floor and plowing into her in a mating frenzy, Rahm lifted his eyes from her glorious mounds to her slender neck which was encircled by a beaded necklace. The necklace had a small string of beads leading from it down between the valley of those delicious peaks.

He roughly jerked his gaze up again. His eyes moved over the slightly rounded chin, to the plush, suckable lips, taking in the most perfect nose, with slightly flared nostrils, before landing on a pair of arctic blue eyes. The contrast between her dark skin and her eyes made them appear even more brilliant in the dim lighting of the bar.

Heat crept up his neck and he gripped the edge of the bar top making indentations in the wood. Those arctic blue eyes were sweeping the bar area, but they'd stopped. They'd stopped on him. Forcing him to grab hold to something to keep his beast under control.

This had just gone from a ten percent moment to a ninety percent —shit—one hundred percent moment between he and his beast. *Fuck!* Rosco was getting punched dead in the face the next time Rahm saw him. It was like his talk of Rahm needing a mate had manifested right before Rahm's very eyes. *Isn't that a bitch?* Literally...

www.ingramcontent.com/pod-product-compliance
Lightning Source LLC
Chambersburg PA
CBHW060641260626
47161CB00008B/2950